Stories by Contemporary Writers from Shanghai

PARADISE
on EARTH

Text by Zhu Lin
Translation by Yawtsong Lee
Cover Image by Getty Images
Interior Design by Xue Wenqing
Cover Design by Wang Wei

Copy Editor: Kirstin Mattson
Assistant Editor: Wu Yuezhou
Editorial Director: Zhang Yicong

Senior Consultants: Sun Yong, Wu Ying, Yang Xinci
Managing Director and Publisher: Wang Youbu

ISBN: 978-1-60220-234-4

Address any comments about *Paradise on Earth* to:
Better Link Press
99 Park Ave
New York, NY 10016
USA

or

Shanghai Press and Publishing Development Company
F 7 Donghu Road, Shanghai, China (200031)
Email: comments_betterlinkpress@hotmail.com

Printed in China by Shanghai Donnelley Printing Co., Ltd.
1   3   5   7   9   10   8   6   4   2

PARADISE
on EARTH

By Zhu Lin

Better Link Press

Foreword

English readers will be presented with a set of pocket books. These books contain outstanding novellas written by writers from Shanghai over the past 30 years. Most of the writers were born in Shanghai after the late 1940's. They started their literary careers during or after the 1980's. For various reasons, most of them lived and worked in the lowest social strata in other cities or in rural areas for much of their adult lives. As a result they saw much of the world and learned lessons from real life before finally returning to Shanghai. They embarked on their literary careers for various reasons, but most of them were simply passionate about writing. The writers are involved in a variety of occupations, including university professors, literary editors, leaders of literary institutions and professional writers. The diversity of topics covered in these novellas will lead readers to discover the different experiences and motivations of the authors. Readers will encounter a fascinating range of esthetic convictions as they analyze the authors' distinctive artistic skills and writing styles. Generally speaking, a realistic writing style dominates most of their literary works. The literary works they have elaborately created are a true reflection of drastic social changes, as well as differing perspectives towards urban life in Shanghai. Some works created by avant-garde writers have been selected in order to present a variety of styles. No matter what writing styles they adopt though, these writers have enjoyed a definite place, and exerted a positive influence, in Chinese literary circles over the past 3 decades.

Known as the "Paris of the Orient" around the world, Shanghai was already an international metropolis in the 1920's and 1930's. During that period, Shanghai was China's economic, cultural and literary center. A high number of famous Chinese writers lived, created and published their literary works in Shanghai, including, Lu Xun, Guo

Moruo, Mao Dun and Ba Jin. Today, Shanghai has become a globalized metropolis. Writers who have pursued a literary career in the past 30 years are now faced with new challenges and opportunities. I am confident that some of them will produce other fine and influential literary works in the future. I want to make it clear that this set of pocketbooks does not include all representative Shanghai writers. When the time is ripe, we will introduce more representative writers to readers in the English-speaking world.

Wang Jiren
Series Editor

Contents

Day 1

Alongside the Rapids of the Fu River

1

The tour bus winding its way through the mountains looks like a tiny goatskin raft adrift in a muddy, wave-tossed sea.

The mountains in northwest Sichuan are ancient—ancient giants bent by age. The terraced loess fields, roughhewn and in dense arrays across the hillsides, worked by generations of farmers, rise like waves from the plains. A hand dipped in the swell will doubtless detect the flow of time, and lives torn asunder may yet be pieced together.

The terraced fields, planted with corn and millet, present a green, regular and timeless, that gleams softly among the folds of the mountains. The swift-flowing Fu River—a sigh breathed by the mountains, a white chain unfurled from above—winds alongside the highway, quietly sniffing the scent of modernity and racing toward civilization without fanfare. This ancient land indeed forms the headwaters of modernity and civilization.

As the passengers ponder, at a motorized speed and in air-conditioned comfort, the meaning of Nature through the window glass, the primitive wilderness makes known its dark desire for greater intimacy. A cold fog closes in on the bus and the rising wind whooshes and roars. In the failing light, road visibility rapidly deteriorates. The Fu River running beside the fog-shrouded road rages and roars a few feet away, a seductive *danse macabre*.

The bus struggles along for a distance before giving up hope of advancing any further. It makes a U-turn and comes to a stop on the level ground of a hollow.

No sooner has the bus stopped than the rain comes pouring down. The passengers breathe with relief, thankful for the experience and prudence of the driver.

Through the bus windows one sees nothing but white sheets of rain; the sky seems to have lightened a bit with the downpour and a dark spot is seen moving in their direction from afar.

At closer range, it turns out to be a child with a swarthy face, dressed in black shirt and pants, leading a white lamb on a leash. He is drenched and all hunched up.

The child breaks into a run toward the bus. Sha Sha, who sits near the door, opens it a crack: "Come in, my child! Come in out of the rain!"

Sha Sha speaks perfectly good Mandarin, albeit with a Taiwanese accent, the kind sported by actors in movies and soaps produced in Taiwan and Hong Kong. But the child seems confused and keeps yelling something in the rain, refusing to get into the bus.

A younger, crisper voice than Sha Sha's speaks up behind her, in a mellow, flawless Mandarin: "Little shepherd, you and your lamb can both come in."

Still unmoving, the child keeps gesticulating with both hands, pointing at the mountain to the right. Sha Sha can't hold the door open any longer because the rain is blowing into the bus, making her heavily made-up face smear like a colorful artist's palette. She hastily closes the door and the yelling of the child is drowned out by the raging wind and pouring rain. All of a sudden a loud rumble, like a peal of thunder, rolls in from the horizon, and Sha Sha lets out a scream as she covers her ears and leans limply into her neighbor.

"Sit back!"

The unexpected sternness in the voice startles Sha Sha and momentarily makes her forget her fear: "Mr. Xu, you..."

Xu Youzhi, in his sixties, is the chief executive of a computer company in Taiwan and Sha Sha's boss.

His eyebrows twitching, Mr. Xu stares grimly at the sheets of rain, as if deciphering, with confident equanimity, a divine revelation.

"Let's move to higher ground fast! A flash flood is going to hit any minute now!" A deep, low baritone voice cries urgently behind Mr. Xu.

"No, let's go back down, let's turn around." Mr. Xu says.

The dark-skinned child has by now darted to the rear of the bus, where he is yelling and waving his arms in the rain.

It finally dawns on the passengers: the danger comes from the mountain in front of them to the right. The bus turns around with some difficulty and moves off at a slow pace, following the lead of the dark child. As he runs ahead, with the lamb at his heels, they look like black and white specks, two dancing beacons in a murky world. The child, with his lamb circling his legs, stops from time to time to wave the bus on.

After about 300 meters, the bus comes to a spot in the lee of a huge rocky overhang that offers protection from the elements. The passengers file off the bus and are led into a spacious, dry cave. A water bottle and a basket sit on the floor, an indication that the child had been staying in the cave a while ago to wait out the rain. So why did he leave the comfort of the cave to wave at the bus in the rain?

The passengers form a circle about the child, asking: "Where are we?" "Is this your territory?"

The swarthy child blinks his eyes but says not a word. He pulls his black upper garment off over his head and removes his black pants, which he wrings to remove the water. Now in the buff he thrashes about like a black fish to shake off the raindrops.

Then they hear the rumble again, like the collective roar of a herd of raging, stampeding bulls.

It comes in waves so loud that the ground shakes and even the bus seems in danger of being thrown off balance. A few hundred meters away—at the spot where the bus had been parked—an avalanche of mud and rocks is cascading down the mountainside like a black waterfall. The mountain has liquefied like a pile of watery mud, instantly creating a new cemetery on the mountain highway.

Everyone stares with disbelief at the cataclysm, jaws dropping. Sha Sha, with tears streaking down her face, bends down to put her arms around the child. She covers his cheek with kisses, creating an abstract painting on the child's rain-slicked skin with her blush, lipstick and eye shadow.

2

When the rain stops and the weather clears, they find the road has been rendered impassible by the mudslide. It is impossible to continue their journey.

Luckily they are prepared for such contingencies. This small tour group of five has brought tents and they decide to pitch camp for the night.

A deep-voiced baritone announces: "Our experiment in the number-axes theory of creative writing starts as of tonight."

The voice belongs to Chen Songlin, a professor in the Department of Chinese Literature at a university in Sichuan, who has for many years devoted himself to the study of the human thought process, using his wonderful brain to think about the wonders of the human brain, diligently tilling the virgin soil of this underexplored area. He has of late become a forceful champion for the marriage of literature and science, proposing a "theory of creative writing based on the concept of number axes" that injects mathematical analysis into literary creation. This has generated interest on the other side of the Taiwan Strait and as a result, Xu Youzhi has flown from Taiwan to mainland China with his secretary to finance and organize this tour for the purpose of testing this creative approach.

When Chen Songlin speaks, a pair of eyes, like two glittering stars, instantly locks onto him—they belong to Li Xing, a graduate student of his who is enamored of his baritone voice.

"Modern society is an information society; information has a life of its own. The replication of information is a type of asexual reproduction incapable of producing new information. Only the cross fertilization of information is sexual reproduction, creating something new. The cross pollination between dissimilar information sets generates vast amounts of new information and ideas.

"The same applies to literary creation. The mechanical re-creation of source materials taken from life is a type of photography. It is a form of asexual reproduction incapable of creating a literary work.

"If we combine different source materials— i.e. information elements—in an orderly fashion, we produce different results from the various permutations. This is how literary conception works. When the combination is optimized, inspiration is generated, which in turn illumines the source materials. When this happens, the writer enters the creative state and produces a literary work. This is sexual reproduction.

"The number-axes approach to literary creation consists of constructing a system of coordinates with the number axes carrying different information elements. The point of intersection of the axes is where the soul of the literary work resides. In order to find that intersection we continually shift the axes, endeavoring to trigger inspirations and capture that glorious moment of union..."

The baritone on whom Li Xing has a crush drones on. According to Xu Youzhi's plan, at the end of the tour, everyone is expected to produce a number of essays conceived and written following the number-axes approach. He, the chief executive, will be exempted from this requirement.

Li Xing is actually paying no attention to what Chen Songlin is saying, for by now she knows by heart the theory he expounds. She may appear to be listening raptly but her thoughts are elsewhere. She is trying to imagine his stage presence when he sings into a microphone while doing karaoke.

She likes to sing this favorite song of hers: "I am a little bird, I want to fly, but hard as I try, I can't soar into the sky. I've been looking and seeking, for a warm bosom on which to lie. Am I aiming too high?"

She has a mellifluous voice but lacks vocal range. Her mentor, on the other hand, prefers to express his thoughts with the aid of his hands instead of his vocal qualities.

To show respect for her mentor, she now wills away the desires crowding her mind and directs her thoughts toward the observations and impressions she has gathered so far on this trip, separating the chaff from the wheat. She is a little nervous. She tells herself there's no need to worry; after all she is the youngest of the lot and it's only natural that allowances will be made for her. But her anxiety refuses to go away: Sha Sha's Mandarin that smacks of movies and soaps from Hong Kong and Taiwan weighs upon her.

She resolves to acquit herself well, even if it means she has to forgo food, drink and sleep. Once her mind is made up, a relaxed look appears on her face and she remarks with false annoyance: "Oh my! That rain storm really scared me witless. Now my brain is a blank and I can't think of anything to write."

"That's all right, it's up to you to write or not to write." Chen Songlin does not insist. He goes on: "It's so beautiful tonight with the moon up. Let's all go out for a walk." As he speaks, his eyes come to rest on her, as though he were seeing the first little star to appear along the evening skyline.

3

"There are so many stars in the sky, so many. But not as many as the sheep in our commune, so many sheep..."

This is a movie theme song that was popular among kindergarten and grade school pupils around the time of Li Xing's birth. The movie, *The Heroic Sisters of the Prairie*, adapted from a real life story, was shown in theaters across China. Even in the old town in the south of the Yangtze River where she was born, that song, in the clear, crisp voice of a child, reigned supreme, the words "xing xing," "stars," carried full blast over public address system.

Her father was squatting on his heels, plucking an old hen, when the midwife ran out of the house announcing: "The sixth child is another baby girl!"

Her father said with a disappointed look on his face: "Let's just call her Xing Xing."

Xing Xing's father went back to hen plucking, which he was doing not to prepare a nutritious meal for the wife who just gave birth, but rather as part of a livelihood on which the whole family depended.

Xing Xing joins her mentor Songlin for a walk;

the night sky, transparent after the rain, is sprinkled
with stars that resemble so many diamonds seemingly
right there for the picking. It's hard for Xing Xing to
imagine that her father was once a straight-A student
in the Department of History of the same university
she is attending. With graduation only a year away,
her father dropped out of school and came home. Her
father's abandon of his studies was a mystery and a
cardinal sin; it remains an enigma to this day, despite
the constant barrages of questions and accusations
leveled by her mother at the dinner table over the
many years.

His family never forgave him for the sin. In those
sweltering summer days her mother, wearing her bib-
like *dudou* over her bare chest, would hurl invectives
across a yard filled with the queer, nauseating, all-
pervading stench of chicken feathers, her two flabby
breasts swinging. At night she would take even the
dudou off and lie face up in the bed, inserting one of
her breasts into father's mouth and emitting cries that
were not any more pleasant to the ears than her verbal
abuse.

Xing Xing completely forgot that she had been
suckled on those same breasts. She was shocked that

her father didn't throw up. She had a good mind to put a torch to the house.

Now, under the starlit sky, the Fu River rushes forth, its surface a white sheet of foam, sending up a frosty spray of water droplets. This is a pristine, unpolluted world.

She has never seen a sky with greater transparency and of a darker blue. The knots of trees, in a variety of shapes and postures, are bathed in the moonlight and show a blue saturated with moisture.

She feels she can gather the sky into her arms but there is no way she can interrupt the headlong rush of the Fu River even for a moment.

The mountains on either bank of the river have been guarding the moving water in stony silence for millennia. But they have not prevented a single drop of water from escaping their custody. As the river flows inexorably on, it is the mountains that have been whittled down by one landslide after another.

In her mind, inspiration strikes like lightning zapping through the clouds; the Rubik's Cube of the Professor's number axes spins through its permutations. These mountains, this river, these stars and the moon above, this night sky, and the rain storm and the mudslide triggered by it are all materials that can be manipulated to create a splendid work. Even a sordid childhood can serve as a dark gray under-painting for the colorful composition.

Xing Xing's eyes glisten with a moist sparkle. Whenever she is overcome with emotion, her iris becomes like a dark purple grape submerged in a pool of transparent water. It's a sight to melt the heart.

4

"Xing Xing!"

"Huh?"

"Xing Xing..."

Chen Songlin has never made a secret of his affection for this girl. For some time now their relationship has been somewhere between a pure mentor-student one and a more ambiguous liaison.

At 54, Chen Songlin still boasts a well-toned physique, a full head of bristly black hair and a firm jaw commonly associated with people given to intellectual debate. But the tough image is tempered by the soft lines around his lips that curve slightly upwards at the corners to give an impression of a permanent gentle smile. When he speaks to a mass audience, this shadow of a smile, combined with penetrating eyes that gleam behind a pair of spectacles, has wowed and conquered many a young woman. In polls taken on the college campuses of the city, he has been rated one of the most charming men by female students.

Chen has argued that modern society is a 3-D society in which three-way relationships should become the norm; a paradigm of such relationships would consist of husband, wife and lover. One can easily imagine him to possess a wife, a child and an apartment occupying an entire floor. The wife might be pretty or virtuous, stodgy or progressive. The couple might be in protracted confrontation over a divorce proceeding. Or the marriage might now exist in name only and the estranged couple may have been quietly practicing the theory of 3-D relationships.

But the fact is Chen Songlin has remained single to this day.

Xing Xing, newly admitted to the graduate program, easily acquired the privilege of unrestricted access to his two-bedroom apartment and of performing janitorial duties therein. But too much should not be read into this state of affairs, for the mentor's acts of intimacy stop at an occasional kiss on her eyes that twinkle like stars.

Xing Xing has proved to be an efficient worker who gets things done and done right. This she has demonstrated in activities ranging from the sorting of information and materials to the transcription of journal articles to household chores such as laundering and cooking. He makes a point of always releasing her well before the dorm for graduate students closes its gate for the night, even when she is in the middle of doing something that badly needs to be done and she is doing a fine job of it.

But she has come to detest the dormitory room containing two wooden beds facing each other. The fat old lady that supervises the dorm building is more than she can stand. She once imagined she would be in heaven the day she left her hometown and that multi-household courtyard reeking of chicken feathers. Now she has learned that the ladder to heaven is long and steep.

She hates the noise in the student cafeteria and pines for the romantic atmosphere of a candlelit restaurant, yet she counts her pennies before parting with her money even for a simple deep-fried pancake. An average college student's monthly spending is around several hundred yuan, and Xing Xing, who does not have the financial backing of her parents and has to work to earn her tuition, takes home a wage that is small change compared to the typical student's allowance.

She fervently hopes to become the better half of the owner of that two-bedroom apartment home. There was speculation that her mentor's celibacy could be due to some kind of male dysfunction. But about a year ago, on a clear cool night in May when she was working late translating some Japanese article for her mentor, he finally proved his perfectly functioning manhood.

One day, not long after that episode, the phone rang when her mentor happened to be out of the apartment. Xing Xing picked up the receiver as if it was the most natural thing to do, only to hear the caller inquire: "Hello, are you Mrs. Chen? We'd like to inform you that your phone account has been the target of identity theft..."

When she later relayed the information verbatim to Chen Songlin, he merely stated matter-of-factly his personal views on phone accounts, with a disconcerting economy of words and facial expressions, not commenting on the caller's mistaken assumption about her status.

Xing Xing briefly felt wronged and unappreciated in the wake of this incident, but she quickly got over it. She is quite insightful and it didn't take her long to understand that she could not physically or mentally remain a prisoner in these two small rooms, stocked though they might be with stacks of books and complete albums of Bach, Mozart, Beethoven and Mendelssohn bought at flea markets in America. These hold an attraction for her but are not enough to hold her in thrall. What does enthrall her is the creamy white answering machine on the desk, a gift from a friend of his in Hong Kong, and the fax machine given by an American friend—these represent a bridge that connects her mentor with the much larger outside world.

She has finally finagled her way onto this bridge, thanks to her mentor, without whom she would not have had the opportunity to become acquainted with the executive from Taiwan. The reason that Mr. Xu has organized this tour is not very clear to her. She has no use for ostensibly noble reasons; all she knows is there's no free lunch in the world. But already she vaguely senses a flicker of hope. Walking cautiously, and with a spring in her step, her head leaning on the broad shoulder of her mentor, she watches the full moon rise, its silvery shine flooding the firmament and, to her, illuminating a soaring bird of opportunity.

5

Mr. Xu, with Sha Sha in tow, takes a different path.

Instead of following the road to the rapids of the Fu River to admire the view, they walk along the highway toward the site of the mudslide.

The moon has risen, the silver moonlight outlining the undulating mountain ranges. The slope hit by the mudslide is coated with specks of black dust—it is coal, created under deep pressure in the earth from dead living matter, which has now come back to the surface, glinting softly and moistly in the silence of the wilderness.

Mr. Xu says: "Moonlight allows man's perception of space to expand beyond the normal constraints.

This walk through the night brings back memories of years long past. Forty years ago I worked as a coal carrier here. And now forty years later I witness all this coal that goes to waste."

Sha Sha looks at him questioningly: "What did you say? Mr. Xu, did you say you'd been here before?"

Mr. Xu cuts short her question with a gesture of his hand: "Don't interrupt me. Write it down, for I also want to write an essay as part of the experiment."

"But I don't have my typewriter with me."

"Write with a pen and a pad."

With a shrug, Sha Sha turns her head slightly to make a face. Mr. Xu goes on: "In 1948 I was in college in Chongqing. I wanted to go to Yan'an to take part in the revolution, and this was the road I took to go north to Yan'an. These are the same mountains and rivers but so much else has changed dramatically, this coal..."

With a quick wave of his hand, he says: "No. What I meant to say is I had a friend then, with whom I share the month and year of birth. Naturally we both have the zodiac sign of the dragon...Hey, Sha Sha, Sha Sha!"

Sha Sha's bursts of laughter rise a distance away,

along a shallow segment of the river littered with smooth white boulders, which is on the hidden, south side of the mound of debris containing coal. She is chasing after the dark little shepherd.

6

"Ha ha, I caught you! I caught you!"

Sha Sha grasps the child by a bare arm, breathless with laughter. A short while ago the members of the tour did everything they could to try to convince the kid to sleep in the tent, talking themselves hoarse and plying him with gifts. As enticement, Sha Sha placed before him all kinds of sweets brought from Taiwan— pineapple tarts, pork floss, almond, pistachios—but he held his ground and would eat only the bread given to him by Chen Songlin, steadfastly refusing to touch the other confections urged on him.

"Hey, why did you come out here alone?"

The child stares at her with his wide-set eyes, uttering not a word, as his lamb rubs itself against his scrawny leg. After the rain the Fu River runs high and murky, its surface has grown wider. The full moon hangs high in the cobalt blue sky and a pristine silence envelops the child, as well as Sha Sha.

In Taipei, the sky is always a dirty gray. There the sun and the moon appear forever to hide behind a veil, as do people's thoughts.

At 33, Sha Sha has had a string of boyfriends, who came and went like passengers getting on and off a city bus, never sticking around for long. And never a single truly ardent, rapturous kiss. Underneath her romantic exterior lies a heart drained of passion. Her friends say to her: "You are fit for displaying in a glass case in the Palace Museum of Taipei."

She merely responds with a smile. No one has guessed the deep hurt behind that smile.

She has taken a great liking to this little shepherd, with his round head, broad forehead, slightly flattened nose and wide lips—an adorable child who mysteriously materialized in the pouring rain to save their lives.

Looking at him, Sha Sha is struck by a sense of having known him. A basic urge attracts her to him: "You want to go home, right?"

Maintaining his silence, the child looks over his shoulder at the flood-damaged bridge over the Fu River.

Sha Sha asks again: "Who else do you have in your home?"

At a slight movement of the child's foot, the lamb emits a bleat. Sha Sha says with a laugh: "I see, you have this lamb for family."

"You are so smart, Auntie."

The clear, well-articulated Mandarin surprises Sha Sha, who attributed his studied silence to his unfamiliarity with anything other than his own local dialect.

She feels impelled to press him on this point: "Who else do you have in your family? Your father? What about your grandmother?"

The child shakes his head vigorously: "I have my yeh yeh, my grandfather on my father's side, with me."

"I see. You live with your yeh yeh. Are you happy?" she blurts out, immediately regretting the silly question. What is happiness? Can she herself give an unambiguous explanation of its meaning?

She changes tack: "What's your name?"

"Ah Long. My name is Ah Long."

"Ah Loong?"

The child has perked up enough to correct Sha Sha's pronunciation, saying in his perfect Mandarin:

"No. It's Ah Long. Yeh yeh gave me that name."

Unhearing, Sha Sha's face blanches as she mutters: "Ah Loong. How odd! He has the same name."

In a mental fog, she sees her Ah Loong again— she is on a date with him, having the time of her life on the backseat of his motorbike, racing up a mountain road. As the trees slide past at a dizzying speed, the pair soars and soars...and her heart soars, expectantly. Finally, when they are under an ancient banyan tree, he circles her waist with his arms, bending down in an awkward attempt to kiss her. She deftly dodges the kiss and says: "You must take a photo of me first."

"Why?" He stares at her uncomprehendingly.

As color rises in her face, she says between bursts of laughter: "I'm told...I'm told that once a girl is kissed by a boy, she is a different person. So, I want you to take a picture of me before the kiss as a souvenir."

"I'll take a picture of you then! I'll take a picture of you!" As he steps backwards with his camera trained on her, he calls out instructions: "Lift your face a little! Lean a bit more this way! Yes, that's perfect! Now smile, smile..."

She puts on the sweet smile of an eighteen-year-old girl for the camera. But the price of their innocent happiness is death—as he edges backward he steps into the void and falls over the cliff.

"Ah Loong, we don't have a home to go back to now. Where can we go except into this vast arch of blue? Let's walk into this infinite space."

Leading the child by his hand, she takes a circuitous route around the river shallows and walks up a mountain trail bordered by shrubs that she doesn't recognize. Their leaves and branches make a soft rustling sound when she parts them. The dark, heavy shadows morph into a fast shifting montage of phantasmagoric shapes that play on her imagination.

When she finally comes to a stop she realizes she and the child are at the edge of a cliff. The Fu River roars a short distance away and the river's surface, reflecting the moonlight, sends off a harsh, cold glint like that of a sword.

Below them lies a pitch-dark, seemingly bottomless gorge, teeming with shadowy masses in all shades of blackness and of varying heights, creating an eeriness that blurs the line between reality and fantasy. In a voice quaking with emotion Sha Sha asks: "Hey, Ah Loong, what's down there? What can you see?"

"Not a thing, Auntie. Go down and see for yourself if you don't believe me."

"All right then, I'll go down. I'm going down!"

As if drawn by a call, Sha Sha walks resolutely into that dark abyss.

7

A cold dampness hovers near the floor of the valley. Branches and leaves lie rotten on a ground covered by slippery moss and strewn with sharp, fang-like stones, all shrouded in darkness. Somewhere a brook murmurs.

The Creator cast this abyss as a timeless enigma, cutting it off from the sunny sky and life-giving hope. Blanched skulls, with soft fertile soil as a pillow, dream of beauty, but are doomed never to see a crimson sunset or an amethyst dawn.

Surprisingly Sha Sha's face exhibits no fear. She gingerly picks her way, exploring her surrounding with both hands and eyes while inhaling a vaguely familiar scent in the eerie darkness.

The child follows behind her leading his lamb on a leash. "Auntie, what are you looking for?"

"I'm looking for a necklace of mine. It's a necklace of beautiful, white, perfectly round pearls."

"When did you drop it here?"

"Oh, a long, long time ago."

"Have you been here before?"

"Yeah, I've been here before."

"When?"

"In my previous life."

"Do you also believe in a previous life, Auntie?" The child adds: "What were we in our previous lives? Were we brothers?"

"Yes, we were brothers, and we loved each other dearly, dearly..." Tears glisten in her heavily made-up eyes. Then, with a shake of her short hair, she purses her lips and starts whistling a tune.

The intermittent whistling seems to have stirred up a black mist, heavy and grotesque, swaying, dancing and twisting as it rises. Dissipated by a sudden gust of wind, it dissolves into countless black raindrops that fall in a fine drizzle and create a long drawn-out, lingering echo as if landing on an ice-cold tombstone.

The echo swells and grows louder, coalescing into a thunderous roar overhead. The child cries with urgency in his voice: "Auntie, let's go back up. The flood is coming down the mountain!"

Sha Sha is startled out of her reverie and, still in a half-awakened state, is dragged by the child toward the rim of the abyss. When they climb to the top of the cliff, she goes limp and plunks down on the ground. The child all of a sudden starts stomping his feet: "Oh no, my lamb, my lamb is still down there!"

As the child gets ready to go back down, the air resonates with an ominous, thundering roar. Sha Sha quickly pulls him back and holds him in a tight grip. "Don't go down! Don't go down!"

"I've got to get my lamb up here." The child sounds desperate.

"Ah Loong, don't...don't go down! Don't even think of it!" Sensing a pending disaster, Sha Sha pleads with the child as her body shivers uncontrollably.

But the child's concern for his lamb trumps all other considerations. Like a slippery mudfish, he wriggles free of Sha Sha and bounds down the steep slope.

As Sha Sha glances down into the dark,

bottomless abyss, her ears are assailed by sounds that seem to come from all directions. It seems she hears jumble of rushing water and human cries for help along with the rumble of mountains quaking. An indistinct white form moves in the distance. It could be a lamb or it could be a giant pearl. The child heads straight for it, in leaps and bounds.

She starts to call after him but finds her voice failing her. Then she hears a shrill lament rise above the thundering roar reverberating in the air: "Ah—Long—"

With this blood-curdling cry, all the water upstream roars down the mountains in a black cascade, instantly turning the valley at the foot of the cliff into a sea.

Sha Sha faints in a heap.

8

"Ah Long—Long—"

As the cry reverberates across mountains and gorges, the ground shakes. Rulan, who has been walking alone, is startled.

She comes to a halt on the narrow trail, her arms hugging her chest. She sees a deep, secluded valley with its far peaks sending up dark billows like the legendary Flaming Mountain. The cry sounds forlorn and pathetic, like the last scream of an expiring life. It interweaves and overlaps with the echoes bouncing off the weathered mountains to form an invisible cyclone. Rulan, a dry leaf swept up in the vortex of sounds, casts about in confusion, searching for the source.

The universe consists of a myriad of discrete systems—from the galaxy to an anthill. And this small tour group is no exception: Chen Songlin and his graduate student form a unit and Sha Sha forms another with her boss, everyone gaining comfort, satisfaction and other benefits from these established relationships—except Rulan, who stands apart, insulated from pleasure and pain, an awkward outsider who doesn't belong.

God, in a moment of nervous distraction, must have unintentionally cast the embryo that was to be Rulan outside all systems—landing at the intersection of a barren weft and an equally barren warp. She became an airborne leaf, buffeted about by unpredictable winds, dragged through muddy waters, and bumped up and down, left and right, across time and space...

When she craved maternal love, her mother became someone else's mother. Standing barefoot in the street, the little girl, tear-stained fingers in her mouth, looked up at towering buildings that formed a canyon lining the street, imagining the warmth and happiness of hearth and home behind one of those windows.

When she pined for the affection of a lover, that lover turned out to be the husband of another woman. As a charming young woman, she again stood in the street, gazing up at the illuminated buildings, vicariously savoring the tender love and ecstasy behind one of those lighted windows.

After a long time, from the ruins of her life, she started to build an edifice she could call her own by enrolling in the writing class of a well-known university in the south. She was already a woman in her forties.

She has joined this tour only because it offered to pay all travel costs. Handing in a few essays presents no challenge to her, although she does not buy the number-axes theory of creative writing. She believes that as a writer, one must give part of oneself as a burnt offering on the altar of creativity. How can one possibly frame the creative process on X- and Y-axes?

She thinks that for Chen Songlin the event provides an opportunity for hype and sensationalism, and that the executive from Taiwan is playing patron of letters because he has money to burn. She, on the other hand, is trying to fit the tenon of her life into a mortise of literature.

To her mind, cutting up one's essay into parts marked by coordinates on axes and then recombining them is like performing an autopsy on a living being. The scalpel may carve out with precision the lungs, the heart and the ribs, but what about blood? Can the surgical knife dissect the blood coursing through the body?

The feelings and emotions that run through a work of literature are thick and warm like blood, pulsating through the work, defying definition by geometry and dissection with a scalpel.

But she is obligated to prove the theory of the number-axes approach with her essays. Her self-esteem and pride will have to be suppressed. After all she is beholden to these people whom she would be wise not to antagonize.

Besides, what assets other than her determination and her intellect does a woman in her forties have to offer up on the merchandise racks of her life?

No wonder she is forever a lonely soul. She is walking all alone in the wilderness; she feels melancholy but also happy.

Communion with nature brings happiness. The trees, finely and crisply outlined by the moonlight, are of a delightful, enchanting green, forming dark networks of branches and leaves. The high peaks and powerful winds contrast with the murmuring brooks and soft breezes, achieving a balance in nature. Rulan can understand the heroic language of the one and the tender whispers of the other.

But all this was ruined by that unexpected, blood-curdling howl, when her soul was swept up by the spiraling cyclone and rudely dropped back into an old nightmare.

In that recurrent childhood dream, her father, looking like a savage with his long hair flowing behind him, searches for her on an uninhabited mountain, calling out as he moves along: "Lan Lan!

Lan Lan!" His calls are echoed back by heaven and earth, amplified into a rumble.

Her father went into hiding during a political campaign in the fifties. Her mother had already divorced him by that time. On the eve of being forcibly taken to Qinghai to receive "reform by labor," he mysteriously disappeared. It was variously rumored that he went to Xinjiang or Yunnan, or snuck out of the country and defected, or even that he was eaten by a tiger in the mountains.

Rulan became an orphan. She was nine.

The thought of finding her father has never crossed her mind. The blurry image she has retained of her father is one who was constantly yelling, if not at her, then at her mother. Her fiery-tempered father never showed a kindly face to her.

Many others who were accused of the same political "crime" as her father did not choose to go into hiding. Instead, true men that they were, they bravely faced up to the consequences of both the political charges leveled against them and their obligations to their loved ones.

But the dream has persisted. Awake, she knows for a certainty that the man in the dream is not her father. But in the dream he invariably becomes her father and she believes without the shadow of a doubt he is her father—that savage with flowing long hair dressed in black.

Now it is all back, that dream, that savage, that father!

He is calling out her name but she does not know where he is. She staggers about, unsure where she is heading, and by the merest chance, stumbles into Sha Sha, who lies on the ground, still unconscious.

The shocking discovery helps her recover her wits, and she hurries to help Sha Sha up, saying: "Sha Sha, Sha Sha! What happened?"

Sha Sha feebly opens her eyes: "Is he...Is he dead?"

"Is who dead?" Rulan is clueless.

"Ah Loong," Sha Sha says, gesturing at a point below them.

Rulan cranes her neck to look down. At the sight of the thundering rapids at the bottom of the gorge she cringes, feeling a flutter in her heart and a weakening in her calves, but soon recovers. "Sha Sha, you're in shock. Let's go. Let's leave this place now."

With all her strength she steadies Sha Sha as they

make their way back toward camp. She displays the calm and composure of an older sister. While Sha Sha is much stronger and stouter than she, at this moment Sha Sha leans on her, totally dependent on her frail frame, which is thin but tough as a willow tree.

After a while she realizes they are on the wrong path and she scans her surroundings to find the way. The moon, low at the northwest corner of the massive mountain, illuminates a rapidly flowing Fu River whose swirling waves throb with a latent vitality, playful as it is savage. At its south bank, it appears as if a gigantic oil painting rises a full five hundred meters above the roaring, turbulent river.

The moment she sees this scene, with dark red motifs on a slate-colored ground, Rulan understands abstraction.

There is a traditional Chinese festival somewhat similar to Valentine's Day, called the "Seventh Evening of the Seventh Moon." On this day, when people, especially young women, look for auspicious signs in the constantly changing clouds, they are usually able to find a dog, a lion, an old man wearing a hat or some other recognizable form.

But here these dark red patterns defy any

morphological associations. If the painting were shrunk to a size of a regular sheet of paper, it would most probably be dismissed as mere scribbles by the hand of a child. However, against the backdrop of a starlit sky, snow-capped mountain peaks and a vast wilderness, its very existence is a mystical, magnificent miracle.

It takes only one look at the scene for Rulan to feel its powerful impact. All the dark red lines and color masses seem to vibrate, dynamically spiraling upwards. There is a sense that a tempest is erupting, in a screaming, stomping rage, from an inner depth.

Sha Sha, awed by the sight, mutters to herself: "What a divine masterpiece!"

Then Rulan becomes aware that the towering oil painting is in reality a sheer rock face. But who could have chiseled these motifs? Who could assert with certainty that this is not a truly great work of art bursting with transcendent wisdom and inner creativity?

She slowly lowers her head and presses her palms together near her heart as if performing some ritual: a prostration before the specter of art, a ritual of communion with an inexhaustible life force.

Suddenly a chill goes through her body and she nearly cries out. She sees him—the father in her dreams—reflected in the shimmering ripples of the raging Fu River, his unkempt long hair blowing in the wind!

9

"Now, we've seen the rapids of the Fu River, the unique topographic features of northwest Sichuan and the wind-eroded formation. I believe everyone has by now acquired a certain amount of material. In order to elevate the use of this material to a higher level, you might consider adding a few coordinate axes. For example, the rain storm and the landslide constitute one axis; the emotions you went through would be another. And the child in the rain, the lamb..."

"Hey, the child! Where is he?"

"The kid has disappeared!"

"How can that be? He was sitting in the tent moments ago, feeding bread to his lamb."

They all talk at once but no one is any the wiser

as to what happened. Presently Rulan remembers something: "I thought I heard a voice calling for Ah Long. It sounded old and desperate. Could it be... someone from the child's family coming to fetch him home?"

"Ah Long? Is the kid called Ah Long?"

Rulan hastens to explain: "I was only guessing. I don't know the kid's name. But someone was calling a name or something. I saw a reflection of the person in the water, and I thought that person might be somewhere up on the cliff. But when I looked up, there was nobody there."

"No, no. There was no child. It was my Ah Loong, my Ah Loong..." The enfeebled Sha Sha suddenly gets agitated. "He followed me in the pouring rain and got us out of danger. I've got to find him."

She gets to her feet and makes for the tent opening but Rulan holds her back. Mr. Xu says, with glaring eyes: "What? What is it? What nonsense is she talking?"

Sha Sha flashes a smile over her shoulder, then making a beeline for Mr. Xu, she puts her hands firmly on his shoulder and executes a pirouette making her silk pants billow out. Before Mr. Xu knows it, a bright red kiss has been planted on his cheek: "Boss, you are so nice! If you had not brought me out here I would never have found my Ah Loong. Thank you so much!"

"Behave yourself! Behave yourself!" Mr. Xu shoves her aside and claws at his face with his hand as though to scratch off the kiss, but the more he scratches, the redder the spot gets. And everyone chuckles with amusement.

But the face of the executive from Taiwan suddenly hardens, and his fingers start to shake. Clearly he has taken serious offense. People exchange silent looks, wondering how things have come to such a pass: the lamb and the child have vanished into thin air, as though they had never existed. Maybe the scene in which they materialized out of the rain was also part of a dream.

The moon hangs low, its light picking out in sharp detail every shrub and every tree on the mountain. The world is like a beautiful iridescent crystal that presents to each spectator a unique colorful facet of itself.

Day 2

On the Back of the Yellow Dragon

1

As the tour bus pulls up in front of the Fu Yuan Lou, the building at the source of the Fu River situated at an elevation of 3,000 meters, there's a stir of excitement in the toasty interior of the vehicle.

Getting off the bus, the passengers walk into a gust of bracing mountain air, and instantly feel its invigorating effect. It is about ten in the morning and the mountains and valleys bask in bright sunshine, which instantly transmits its friendly warmth to the skin. But there is an unmistakable nip in the air; a chill-laden wind trundles through the sun-drenched landscape, creating a sharp contrast to the warmth of the sun.

They come to a pond, its surface wrinkled by the wind. Chen Songlin squats down on his heels and dips a towel in the water. With the wetted towel he starts rubbing his face. Seeing that he is clearly enjoying this, the ladies are quick to follow his example. But the moment they stick their fingers in the water, they flinch as if bitten. Xing Xing lets out a sharp cry: "Yow! It's so cold!" Rulan, though not making a sound, also feels as if her bones were jabbed by a steel needle. The water is uncommonly cold.

Only Mr. Xu does not linger. He walks on, hands clasped behind his back, along a path that leads past the pond toward the Fu Yuan Building. "That's snow water. It's unfit for bathing."

The serious look on his face gives him an air of someone who knows best. Quickly shaking off the drops of water from her fingers, Xing Xing trips along to catch up with him, and the rest of the company follows closely behind.

While the Fu Yuan Building is called a *lou*, which implies a multi-story building, it is actually a traditional wood-framed one-story structure with red eaves and a black-tiled roof. Its interior walls and roof are devoid of ornate decorations, and its simple, stark design lacks both the bold strokes of the northern architectural style and the subtlety and refinement of the southern style.

Once inside the building, the first thing that greets the eye is a clear stream flowing under the structure. Its murmuring sound is soothing to the ears. The visitors note enthusiastically: "Oh, so this is the source of the Fu River!"

When they look at the structure itself, they are struck by the wisdom and ingenuity of its original architect. Only the Chinese could have come up with the idea of erecting a structure to enclose this little spring so high up. They all agree that this unprepossessing building deserves to be called the premier building in all of China.

They exit the other end of the small building to be greeted once again by a cloudless blue sky, so blue and so transparent that these visitors from big cities instinctively narrow their eyes for fear of sullying that pristine purity. Fluffy masses of clouds hang low, floating like a boa at mid-height around the hills, fixed in place and in shape, proud to have the vast sky all to themselves.

While the chilly wind and the blazing sun go

about their respective business, they also work in harmonious collaboration, and the ubiquitous pine forests break into a lush green under the stimulus of this combination of cold and warm forces. Strong gusts of wind blowing through the pine trees create a continual, surf-like sound.

Sha Sha, who has been quite listless so far, is springing back to life. "Wow, are these pine trees? There are so many of them, so many! I am seeing them for the first time, the very first time! There is not a single pine tree to be found in downtown Taipei."

Whipping out her camera she starts photographing the pine trees, which come in a variety of shapes and postures. She is all over the place, running this way and that, climbing up and climbing down.

Xing Xing feels it's a pity that Sha Sha is taking pictures only of the trees. What a waste of film! The same pictures would have an added sentimental value if Sha Sha posed in them.

Xing Xing loves to have her picture snapped but she doesn't have a camera and has never spent money on picture-taking, although she does own a thick album crammed full with photos.

Sha Sha's enthusiasm has rubbed off on her. The magnificent landscape with its bright light and unique colors give Xing Xing an urge to have a dozen pictures taken of her. But she doesn't want to have to ask Sha Sha for that favor no matter how strong her desire to have those pictures. Of course, if Sha Sha should read Xing Xing's mind and volunteer to take a few pictures of her, she would gladly accept the offer.

But Sha Sha has never concerned herself with other people's thoughts, especially not in her present state of excitement. With her camera slung over her neck, she scurries about snapping pictures almost without thinking, from time to time popping into her mouth a green tablet, which she chews with a crunching sound and which leaves a green stain on her red lips.

Rulan is acting curiously out of character: she follows Sha Sha about, offering pointers every so often: "Look! That tree has a nice shape! Sha Sha! Come over here! This is a perfect angle!"

This has the effect of fanning the enthusiasm of Sha Sha, who compliments Rulan after every shot: "You really have a knack for choosing the right scene!"

Or else: "Don't move! Stay there as background for the photo!"

Xing Xing blushes for Rulan. She thinks this woman in her forties has brought shame on all mainlanders. The normally phlegmatic and eccentric Rulan is demonstrating an uncharacteristic haste when it comes to fawning over this young lady from Taiwan.

It occurs to her that she should remind Chen Songlin to use his camera to take a group photo, as is normally done for such organized events.

For some reason Chen Songlin appears a little subdued, not his usual self today. After exiting the Fu Yuan Building, he has quickened his pace and left the others behind. Normally it would only take a glance from Xing Xing for him to know it is time to snap a picture of her.

As Xing Xing is about to call after him, she suddenly hears Mr. Xu say with a frown in the direction of Sha Sha and Rulan: "Enough already!"

She swallows her words. Sha Sha comes running toward Mr. Xu, camera in hand, and shouts joyously: "It is great! It is so great! Mr. Xu, have you ever seen pine trees before?"

"Don't be ridiculous! Have I ever seen pine trees indeed!" The old man makes a gesture of disgust with his hand and walks on ahead.

The rebuke is just water off a duck's back to Sha Sha, who retorts good-humoredly: "Can't you be a little nicer to a young lady?"

"Silly!" Mr. Xu says petulantly, quickening his pace to catch up with Chen Songlin.

Chen Songlin slows down for Mr. Xu, who is a little out of breath, saying: "Take it easy! There is less oxygen at this high altitude."

Pointing at his head, Mr. Xu says with a sigh: "I had no idea she was messed up here. Well, it's that society she lives in!"

Chen Songlin knows he is talking about Sha Sha, and he hastens to assure him: "Mr. Xu, don't you worry! I've asked Rulan to take care of her."

"But Sha Sha's duty is to take care of me!" Not caring if he's overheard by those following them, he allows a note of exasperation to enter his rising voice: "Do you know how high her monthly salary is? And how much this tour is costing me? I've hired a high-priced...fruitcake! I feel really lousy."

"Why don't you let Xing Xing take care of you?"

Chen Songlin says with a chuckle.

A grunt has barely escaped Mr. Xu's throat before Xing Xing insinuates herself between the two men. With her head cocked to one side and her arched smiling eyes blinking, she says: "Mr. Xu, we are a socialist society, so we take care of one another. You need not pay me a salary."

Looking at this girl with a fetching smile and a sweet disposition, Mr. Xu smiles in return, blinking his myopic eyes and saying: "Good! Good! Very good!"

2

A dragon! A yellow dragon!

The three women, who couldn't be more different from one another in temperament, cry out with one voice as they stop short and look up simultaneously.

The exclamation is followed by an awed silence, with all of them holding their breath.

A giant yellow dragon—a full five hundred meters wide—snakes up the undulating blue mountains amidst the roar of cascading waterfalls. It reaches toward a distant peak, extending as far as the eye can see, its head lost in the skyline.

"This is the result of the sedimentation of calcium carbonate," Chen Songlin explains, pointing at the yellow torso of the dragon. "For millennia lime-bearing water has deposited calcium carbonate on the riverbed, leaving a yellow hue and creating this spectacular yellow dragon."

No one pays attention to Chen Songlin's explanation; even Xing Xing is silent. Before such a spectacular wonder of nature, these travelers exploring the wilderness are seized by a dreamlike enchantment and care little for scientific explanations.

Rulan puts her arm through Sha Sha's and Sha Sha puts her arm around Xing Xing, the three women the picture of sisterly affection. The moment of shared emotion brings a pure unadulterated happiness.

The foaming water tumbles down the back of the yellow dragon, sending up a fine mist that catches the highland sunlight with the brilliance of thousands of tiny diamonds. The white bubbles whipped up by the fast flowing water are like glittering armored scales that form part of the trappings of the dragon's power.

"Look! Doesn't it resemble a giant dragon flying

through the air?" Mr. Xu asks in a loud, excited voice.

The three women respond in unison: "We are descendants of the dragon!" They know it's not true but they can't help feeling proud to be associated with such a powerful creature.

They climb the steps; the mountain is not particularly steep and they take their time in a slow ascent. The dragon, although it appears to be flying, has not lifted off the ground, its winding magnificence solidly anchored to the mountains.

Probably to protect the dragon, wooden boardwalks have been built over the water flowing down its back. Further up, when one looks off into the distance, the head of the dragon can be seen just beneath the summit of a far mountain. Against the blue sky and among the snowy peaks, the dragon appears to be lord paramount of time and space.

Chen Songlin explains that this "dragon" is several kilometers long and its "head" rises 3,600 meters above sea level. He repeatedly reminds Mr. Xu to keep his medications with him, but Mr. Xu turns a deaf ear. So he leaves the oxygen pouches brought up for the ascent in Xing Xing's care in case they are needed.

"This dragon is me," says Mr. Xu all of a sudden. "My name is Yun Long, which means cloud dragon."

Sha Sha gives him a startled look: "But your name is Xu Youzhi!"

"Don't interrupt me." Mr. Xu waves an impatient hand. "Anyway I was once called Yun Long. I was in college, and there was another 'dragon' in my class, and he was a yellow dragon because his surname was Huang, yellow. His first name was Gu Long, ancient dragon. We were both active in the student movement and later...we were blacklisted. We had to go into hiding because the authorities were after us. This is the road I took when I was on the run. There is a temple in this mountain, where Huanglong Zhenren, the Yellow Dragon Immortal, is worshipped."

"And there is a cave near the temple," Chen Songlin adds, "called Huanglong Cave—Yellow Dragon Cave. This cave is so deep that some say it links to the city of Chengdu. Some even claim it leads all the way to heaven."

The two men break off there, leaving the rest to the ladies' imagination.

Xing Xing says with a silly, fascinated expression

on her face: "Go on, go on with your story!"

Mr. Xu looks at her with a smile: "Look! Look at the dragon! I've been to many places in the world but I've never seen anything more beautiful than this dragon and this stream flowing on its back! See those dragon claws over there?"

Indeed, on the rock faces on either side are giant, gnarled yellow marks, raised in relief, looking very much like a dragon's claws.

Xing Xing runs over with a cheer and starts playfully stamping her feet on those sacred dragon claws. This puts Mr. Xu in an even jollier mood: "I say! This dragon symbolizes the rise of the Chinese nation. This is a perfect shot. Take a picture! Take a picture now!"

3

On the trail going up the mountain, Xing Xing has many a picture taken of her together with the abundant flowers. The white and red flowers blanketing the hills have heavy petals that vibrate with life and passion, unlike more demure specimens growing on the plains.

Xing Xing insists on being educated, asking: "Mr. Xu, what kind of flower is this?"

Mr. Xu, who seems to have an answer for everything, keeps silent. Luckily Chen Songlin comes to the rescue: "This species is called *Rhododendron watsonii.*"

"Professor Chen, have you also been here before?"

Chen Songlin finds this velvety voice comes from Rulan. He marvels at her sensitivity and unusual perception. But he sidesteps the question: "Plants form part of the environment. Those growing in the fertile soil of the plains and receiving plentiful rain and sunshine will, like people living a sheltered life, have a well-shaped and developed exterior but are actually quite delicate and vulnerable. Trees growing near the seashore and in the fissures of rocks develop a resilience that comes from their struggle with an adverse environment, not unlike people who are made tough by a harsh life. Here these rhododendrons scratch out an existence defying the cold and the high altitude. Their flowers can turn from white to red with changes in the climate."

Indeed, the flourishing rhododendrons on either

side of the boardwalk already appear to overrun the claws and the torso of the dragon. Their brilliant colors herald spring on the highland and their flamboyant aggressiveness seemingly threatens to engulf the dragon in flames.

They have by now climbed for more than an hour. They can see neither the head nor the tail of the "yellow dragon." The water trickling down its spine catches the noontime sunlight, giving off a golden glitter that makes the dragon appear ready to fly off into space.

Mr. Xu says: "Already back then I felt that China was a dragon lying low among these snow peaks and that it would take off one day. At the time, I was so excited that I went up the mountain to prostrate myself before the Yellow Dragon Immortal, and inform him that I too was taking off..."

He is cut off in mid-sentence by Sha Sha's cry: "Oh, look! We are almost at the top."

And indeed they see ahead of them a snow-clad peak. Excitement grows among the travelers, who believe that this may be the snowy summit they sighted previously. But Mr. Xu bursts into laughter: "Who says we are near the top? Look! There are more mountains beyond this. There are mountains and there are mountains."

"It's true. There is another bigger snow peak behind this one," says Xing Xing.

"Of course! Where do you think all this water comes from? It's from the big snow peak!" Mr. Xu wags his head in smug satisfaction.

"Does the peak have a name?" Xing Xing asks.

"It's called Min Mountain, my child." Mr. Xu explains with great patience, "In high school, you must have read the famous verse lines by Mao Zedong about crossing Min Mountain's miles of snow. What a sweeping landscape his words conjured and what boldness of vision!"

"Ah, now I understand!" Xing Xing says with a happy laugh. "The source of the Fu River is Huanglong Ravine, the yellow dragon, and the water of Huanglong Ravine comes from the Min Mountain."

Rulan adds: "But the Fu River is a very small river. The melted snow of the Min Mountain also feeds into other rivers, including the Min, the Jinsha, the Dadu and the Yangtze."

Mr. Xu nods in grave agreement. "The melted

snow from these high mountains has nurtured Chinese civilization."

The group stops for a brief rest. Under the bright, blue sky, white clouds hover around the pristine snow peaks. Pine trees inscribe lush green lines on the hills, above which a lone eagle flies soundlessly.

"That snow peak is called Xue Baoding," Mr. Xu says. "In antiquity there was a beautiful Tibetan girl called Xue Baoding. Two young men—Sangga and Qiubu—fell in love with her. Sangga and Qiubu were both accomplished horsemen and archers as well as outstanding warriors. They were both handsome and strongly built. Xue Baoding had a hard time deciding which of them she loved more."

"That's impossible," Sha Sha protests. "If she loved one, then she couldn't possibly also love the other."

The remonstrance causes Mr. Xu's eyebrows to rise, so Xing Xing hastens to lighten the atmosphere: "You never know. Human affection is complex and it's hard to really know one's own mind."

The cloud lifts from Mr. Xu's face and he continues his story-telling: "Sangga and Qiubu were very close friends and Xue Baoding did not have the heart to hurt either of them. So she had them compete in a contest of martial skills on the big marshy grassland, with the winner taking her as bride. The two young men hopped on their horses and engaged each other with their swords. They fought to a draw but all of a sudden Qiubu's horse slipped and fell forward, throwing him directly onto the sword of Sangga before he could draw it back. With a pained cry, Qiubu fell in a pool of blood as the sword slit his throat. Seized with grief and guilt, Sangga drew an arrow from his quiver and plunged it into his own chest.

"Both young men died, their blood dyeing the grassland red. Xue Baoding went up the mountains to live in seclusion, never to marry, and eventually she turned into that peak over there, far from the civilized world."

After hearing Mr. Xu's story, the travelers take a fresh look at the peak, their imagination conjuring a beautiful lady floating in the air.

"Xue Baoding is shrouded in clouds and mists year-round, demurely hiding her face behind them. It's only in the bright sunshine of May that we have a chance of seeing her true face, but, but..."

Mr. Xu's voice drops to a murmur and another, softer voice seamlessly continues in an undertone: "But we can never see into her heart. Who does she love? Who does she love more?"

It is Rulan who is speaking, composed and serene, more to herself than to the others, without meaning to be heard. In fact no one has paid any heed, except Mr. Xu, who jerks his head around to look with astonishment at her—this is the first time since the start of the tour that he has taken a close look at this shadow-like, quiet woman.

Rulan is a little discomfited by his attention and politely averts her gaze, but not before detecting in his eyes a dark shadow, a shadow that had been dissipating with the passage of time but that has reconstituted itself. She senses a profound hurt hidden deep down in his heart. His appearance of jocularity and his outgoing disposition is but a front, she believes. Although he is tall and stoutly built, his back is already stooped. Especially now, whether out of fatigue or low spirits, or the lack of oxygen at high altitudes, the rosy color of the cheek, which is an indication of good health, has given way to an earthy look. She even detects a slight unsteadiness in his gait, as if he were an elderly man, an ageing father, who needs a steadying hand.

The thought brings a slight frown to her brow and she briefly fixes her beautiful, sad eyes on him. If he were a ragged old peasant from the mountains, or an impoverished teacher, she would probably go up to him, put her arm through his and whisper a few gentle words to him, hoping this quiet exchange could melt but a tiny bit of the sadness and wretchedness burdening each of their hearts.

But he is a rich executive from Taiwan, who swims in money, owns a thriving business and is surrounded by beautiful young ladies. In a world of ubiquitous suffering and misfortune, why should she concern herself with the pain of a rich executive from Taiwan?

She turns her eyes away from him and starts off alone.

4

When they reach the calcified pool named Zhenhai, Stone Pagoda Pool, near the top at 3,500 meters above sea level, they find the air thin and cold. But orchids of the species *Cypripedium fargesii* in red, yellow and violet are everywhere, growing in the moraine soil or distributed among the shrubs, filling the air with a fresh scent of wild mint. Stretching as far as the eye can see are mineral pools of myriad sizes and shapes, some large, some small, some square and some round.

The chain of pools of clear, turquoise water is bounded by naturally curved embankments, rising up the mountain like a crystal staircase to the blue firmament. Looking closely one will find that the pristine clarity of these pools is a mirror image of the blue serenity of the vast universe.

Rulan is all of a sudden seized by a sense of having come home. The feeling hits her with astonishing speed and force.

She had been walking at the head of the group but now slackens her pace and falls back. Her vague sense of déjà vu and nostalgia has become more concrete, the proverbial hesitancy of a long absent native coming closer to home. She cannot help feeling scared, scared that she might refuse to come back down the mountain. She might decide to stay here, becoming a sapphire droplet of water in these pools and a lifelong companion to Xue Baoding, sworn to a life of seclusion in the highland.

Has she searched for forty-odd years, never finding true love in human society, only to return to Nature, to the source of all things, to this pool of simple blue?

Sha Sha has a sudden inspiration. She says cheerfully, pointing at the clear blue water: "Rulan, Rulan. The first part of your name *ru* is a pun on 'as,' and *lan*, means 'blue'! As blue as you!"

Those words sound like thunder to her ears, and Rulan feels her blood surging through her body. She feels as though she were going through the thrill of a rebirth.

"Rulan, it's only when I got here and saw the Stone Pagoda Pool that I've come to fully appreciate the beauty of your name and the...the peculiarity of your personality. You appear aloof but deep down you are a tender soul. You may have been through a lot of suffering, but you are able to leave room for purity and innocence in a corner of your heart. A beautiful blue, the color of the sky: it purifies body and mind and soothes the suffering soul..."

Sha Sha has taken a liking to Rulan either because the latter has taken solicitous care of her throughout the trip or because they shared a good time taking pictures. She chatters on in her Taiwanese accent, evidently proud of the way she throws in poetic vocabulary. Rulan's attempts to interrupt her have the opposite effect, further whetting her enthusiasm. She rattles on, tactlessly: "They say character determines destiny. I say your name determines your character. But why did your father and mother give you a name like that? Is it because they visited this place?"

"Sha Sha! Stop blabbering!"

To Rulan the mention of her so-called father and mother is taboo. She never talks about them with anyone, and people who know her are aware of this, taking great care to steer clear of the subject. But this young lady from across the Taiwan Strait, blithely ignoring the clouds gathering in Rulan's face, puts her arm around her.

"Hee hee! I am not blabbering. Listen to me! I suspect your father and mother made love here under this blue sky and conceived you, the blue-sky daughter. At your conception you received the best of the delicate beauty of nature and the finest the sun and the moon have to offer. Hey, you..."

It's not that she has suddenly realized her lack of tact or that Rulan has had an unusual reaction. Sha Sha is simply startled by her own ability to run off at the mouth like that. She studies Rulan intently, her eyes moving from the loose-fitting light blue wool sweater to the deep blue jeans that bring out her tall slenderness, to the white sneakers, and the white and blue comb holding her long hair in place. She realizes with a start that this graceful woman is dominated from top to bottom by a blue-and-white theme. She wonders why it escaped her notice when they were taking all those pictures.

Rulan does not wear designer clothes or accessories but the casual simplicity sets off her subtle elegance, which Sha Sha finds adorable. She even feels that Rulan's oval-shaped face, which has lost the rosy hue of youth, is somehow very familiar, a face that she has seen somewhere.

"Rulan! Rulan!" Putting her fingers to the other's exposed neck, she feels the smoothness of her skin. "I find that human beings are really mysterious, frighteningly mysterious."

5

Sha Sha's speech falters and a rapt expression appears on her face. While she resents Sha Sha's indelicate rambling, Rulan has been drawn despite herself into a strange trance-like state.

Lightning streaks across the dark clouds and there is no telling where the thunderclap will fall.

"Huang Rulan. Since her surname is Huang, how can you name her Rulan? 'Yellow as blue'? This is absurd! It has to be changed. Change her name and resubmit the enrollment form!"

"What name do you suggest?"

"Huang Huifang, Huang Xiuqin, Huang Yuyin... Huang anything for all I care, but not Huang Rulan."

"No! I am her mother and I insist on calling her Rulan."

"But she has the surname of the Huang family!"

"Do you really think the blood of the Huang family runs in her?"

Pop!

A loud slap landed on the woman's face; that

white, delicate face was the last impression Rulan had of her mother. The rest is shrouded in a blurry fog.

Rulan's father came from a landlord background and cared for his old mother at home. The matriarch kept clamoring for a grandson to keep alive the Huang lineage. Her mother, on the other hand, was a self-styled progressive who would see nothing wrong in changing even the surname of her daughter.

As far as Rulan can remember she was never picked up, kissed or cuddled by anyone when she was little. Neither her father nor her mother cared to look at her. It's as if she had become the collateral damage of their argument over her naming, which had for no good reason made her the focus of their resentment.

Her name "Rulan" appears in a famous Tang dynasty poem she learned in elementary school. The poet describes in glowing terms the beauty of Jiangnan—what is today the Jiangsu and Zhejiang area—describing how the flowers along the Yangtze banks blazed fiery red when the sun was up and the river water turned "as blue" in spring.

It is a poem that flows easily off the tongue, crisp and bright. But the colorful spring scenes it celebrates in no way paralleled the life of a little girl named Rulan from Jiangnan.

The year she turned twenty she was carrying buckets of water up a hill in the Huai river basin as part of a mass campaign to rescue the soybean plants dying in the fields. People worked hard day and night to salvage as much as they could during one of the great droughts. She went into the field despite suffering from malaria, and fainted with a high fever in a parched, cracked irrigation ditch. The pole used for carrying the water buckets fell off her shoulder and the buckets filled with water overturned. When she woke up it was already midnight. She had a great thirst and desperately needed a drink of water! But all she saw was the gaping, parched mouth of the earth with its black fangs. Nobody was there to offer assistance or to help her up, so she had to crawl inch by inch toward her lodging—that cow shed of the production brigade...

Waking from her reveries, Rulan takes another look at the terraced pools and realizes that they are not uniformly blue. Those that receive the most direct sunshine display a spectrum of colors: light yellow, violet, emerald green, indigo blue—the chromatic profusion is as alluring as the sweet juices of fresh fruit.

The group's awed silence is broken by Xing Xing's cry of wonder: "Look at those trees growing in the water!"

Indeed trees in a variety of poses populate the pools; some stand gracefully in the water, some have quietly grown at an angle and expanded beyond the embankments, while still others lie recumbent or submerged in water. With their tender new leaves ruffling the water surface and the gnarled old roots washed by the clear streams, these trees are so well irrigated that they display a brighter, more transparent green and greater grace than plants growing on land.

Chen Songlin patiently points out: "This is a Euphrates poplar and that one is a water willow." But the explanations are mostly ignored by the rest of the group, who curiously study the submerged trunks and roots. Some of them, they find, have acquired a coat of calcified deposits, giving them the allure of deep sea corals and adding vivid colors to the terraced pools.

The travelers brought before this spectacular landscape experience a feeling of having entered a world of magic. Then they are startled out of their dreamy state by yet another of Xing Xing's joyous cries: "Mr. Xu! Isn't that the Huanglong Temple you talked about?"

Rulan looks up and sees a temple of an unimpressive height situated on a hillock not far away. Together the group starts off toward the building. But Mr. Xu plumps himself down on the ground, saying to the others: "You go ahead. I'd like to rest for a while."

"Mr. Xu! Come with us! Don't you want to pay a visit to the Yellow Dragon Immortal?" Playfully pleading, she tries to drag him up. Mr. Xu waves his hand, a look of dejection on his face. "There may not be much to see there. Anyway I am tired."

Xing Xing decides to stay and sits down beside him to keep him company.

Sha Sha enters the temple with Rulan close behind, and they find a half life size statue of a bearded old man on the altar—it must be the Yellow Dragon Immortal.

The temple turns out to be quite rundown and small, and a walkthrough has turned up nothing worth seeing. They emerge from the temple rather disappointed. It's then that they realize Chen Songlin has disappeared.

They find a lichen-covered trail leading into a dense wood. The ground, carpeted by spongy soil about seven or eight inches deep, is soft under their feet. Sha Sha gets excited and insists on exploring further, so there's nothing for Rulan to do but follow her.

In the immense forest a scent of decayed wood and mushrooms floats in the air. As they venture deeper into the woods they see clumps of beard lichen hanging from tall pine and fir trees, countless green nets woven into a dark labyrinth.

The green veils of lichen sway in the wind, sending a chill up Rulan's spine. Clutching Sha Sha by the arm, she says: "Let's turn back. We don't want to get lost in the woods."

Barely have her words died down than a grave, faraway voice is heard above the low surf-like sound of the wind in the woods, crying: "Ah Long—"

It's a familiar voice, an old man's voice, at the sound of which color drains from Sha Sha's face.

Shocked, Rulan opens her mouth but before she can say anything, Sha Sha has already broken away and is running deeper into the woods. Rulan anxiously calls after her. But Sha Sha's headlong dash is unstoppable. The green veils sway overhead, seeming to cast a shroud over the entire woods.

6

"She's nuts! Her conduct is beyond the pale!"

Mr. Xu has become entirely agitated and distraught at the news of Sha Sha's escapade in the woods. Luckily Chen Songlin has reappeared in the nick of time. He instructs Xing Xing to take Mr. Xu down to their bus while he himself sets out with Rulan to look for Sha Sha.

Sha Sha left her backpack in the empty lot in front of the temple before dashing off, probably thinking she would come back for it. There is no choice but to carry it, the bulging backpack weighing heavily on the small frame of Xing Xing, who looks overwhelmed.

Mr. Xu says with a frown: "Throw it away! It's not as if it has any treasures in it. Not worth breaking your back for it."

Xing Xing would be only too glad to be rid of the

burden, but she answers without a hint of bitterness: "It's all right. I'm fine." Then she adds with a chuckle: "Maybe Sha Sha does have some precious stuff in it."

Mr. Xu, grim-faced, feels the pack with his hand and says with a snort: "I knew she'd pack this thingamajig!"

"What thingamajig?" Xing Xing, by now breathless with the heavy load on her back, still manages to flash a winning smile as she asks with great interest.

Mr. Xu gives a description, gesturing with his hands: "It's something long and round."

As Xing Xing follows the hand gestures with her eyes, a spot of color comes into her cheek. Mr. Xu says with a wink: "A water purifier!"

Xing Xing breathes with relief, remembering that wherever they go Sha Sha always filters water by shaking it in a clear cylindrical container before drinking it. That must be the gadget she's carrying on her back now.

She resents the fact that she, a graduate student, should perform this kind of menial labor for a superficial, less educated young woman like Sha Sha. But her face betrays no emotion. "Sha Sha said she was warned before leaving Taiwan that the water in mainland China is undrinkable and her folks had prepared bottles of mineral water for the trip. She would have lugged them all the way to China (the mainland) too if not for the weight it would add to her luggage."

This sounds like a defense of Sha Sha's behavior, and it only upsets Mr. Xu more: "Billions of Chinese (mainlanders) drink the water without a problem, why can't she? It's a bunch of nonsense!"

"She seems to believe she has come to a savage land of primitives," Xing Xing humors him along. "She has brought two bunches of chopsticks, not to mention a large supply of plastic bowls."

"Pathetic!" Mr. Xu says dismissively.

"Are all young women in Taiwan like this?" Xing Xing asks, blinking her eyes innocently.

"How can that be possible?" He is furious. "On the other hand I'd say she's quite typical. It's just my rotten luck!"

"In that case, why..." Xing Xing's voice trails off.

Mr. Xu smiles widely: "Nosy girl! You want to know why I keep her as my secretary, right? Let me explain. Although she is an employee of my company,

I really know nothing of her past."

Seeing that Xing Xing has not been entirely convinced, Mr. Xu adds: "That's how it works in our part of the world. The company doesn't pry into things that have nothing to do with work. One doesn't even really know one's own daughter, much less a young lady working in the office."

"Really?" Xing Xing is intrigued.

"It's a fact," says Mr. Xu. "There was this guy who visited a brothel. He picked one girl from the video catalog and in the course of chatting with the girl he found out she was actually his own daughter."

"How could that be?" Xing Xing cries out.

"Well, it was a daughter by a mistress of his. Since the daughter didn't grow up in his household, he really had no idea what she looked like." Mr. Xu sighs again as he explains: "It's a commodity society, where money reigns supreme and anything goes, no matter how despicable and depraved, as long as there's money to be made. Upscale hotels provide naked hostesses; some hotels are reserved for lady guests only. Some couples go to Turkish bathhouses, the husbands and wives going their separate ways once inside to look for other partners of the opposite sex with total freedom—that shows you to what depths of decadence and debauchery people have descended! Sometimes dozens of people, male and female, meet up to inhale superglue. It's frightening! It's almost like the coming of apocalypse."

It is with a spring in her step and a bright smile on her face that Xing Xing listens to Mr. Xu's description of the "apocalypse," almost forgetting the heavy weight on her back. "Mr. Xu, it's really a pity. You should have come to the mainland earlier."

Casting a sidelong glance at her, Mr. Xu detects a sly, naughty look in the smiling eyes of this young woman. He smiles also, asking: "Should I have?"

"You really should have!" Xing Xing answers without hesitation. "When I was in third grade, the teacher planned a meeting devoted to the subject of class struggle. It was my duty as class president to help the teacher find someone to make a presentation to the class about the abysmal misery of our Taiwanese compatriots..."

"Naughty girl!" Mr. Xu realizes he's been made a fool of by this mischievous young lady, and puts on an angry, menacing look. Giggling, Xing Xing runs off into a patch of pine trees bordering the boardwalk with Mr. Xu in pursuit. He seems to have shed twenty years all of a sudden.

7

Upon seeing Xing Xing for the first time, no one would ever describe her with terms so much in vogue nowadays such as "sexy" or "sculpted." Her unimpressive height, her slenderness and her lack of curves give her the appearance of a girl whose body has not fully developed. But there is a clean sweetness to her oval-shaped face, and the expressive dark eyes under her ordinary brows seem so eloquent. She has "double eyelids," the type of wider lid with a crease thought desirable by many, as well as long eyelashes, irises with an amber twinkle, and an endearing air of having just been woken from a reverie. She is sometimes lethargic while at other times she doggedly tries to accomplish some trivial thing, showing a single-mindedness often found in children.

Once in the woods, Mr. Xu has the whim of collecting some plant specimens as souvenirs. She immediately shrugs off the backpack and starts scouring the area for leaves of various colors, which she brings to Mr. Xu for examination. After closely inspecting these leaves with their diverse shapes, Mr. Xu can barely contain his admiration, saying: "These highland plants are so beautiful! Look at those exquisite lines suggesting the waviness of water!"

Xing Xing listens, with her clear eyes widened in child-like curiosity, to Mr. Xu's effusive praise and starts nodding as if in sudden enlightenment: "And they express the tenacity, nobility, dignity and fragility of life. Their beauty is an unspoiled beauty of creation."

Mr. Xu turns his head to look with amazement at her. "You have such a pleasant voice."

Xing Xing beams with delight, her eyelashes fluttering and her amber eyes shining. Her face lights up as the color rises in her cheeks. "Then shall I sing a song for you?"

Taking no notice of her, Mr. Xu puts a hand to his forehead. "You've stirred up many memories. I remember there is a kind of fern growing here whose roots are edible when ground into a powder."

"Mr. Xu, I'll dig one up for you." Xing Xing trips away, her faded carnation-colored jacket floating about like a fluffy cloud in the ancient conifer forest. Xu Youzhi plunks himself down at the base of a tree and idly strokes the leaves of a shrub with his hand. Flashes of memory come back to him. He can almost hear that little girl's wistful singing: "I am a little bird, I want to fly, but hard as I try, I can't soar into the sky..."

Looking up, he sees Xing Xing holding out a sprig of fresh green fern, her delicate hands caked with mud. "Mr. Xu, is this the fern you were talking about?"

Her cheeks are flushed, beads of perspiration glisten on her forehead, and her dense, soft long hair, which normally hangs down to her shoulders, has been braided into two pigtails that are rolled up and pinned behind her ears. She has the air of a village maid with a basket on her arm out to dig wild vegetables.

Xu Youzhi beams with delight: "Let me take a look!"

"Not unless you give me some dollar bills!" Xing Xing playfully hides the fern behind her back.

"No problem," Xu Youzhi readily agrees. "Is one dollar enough?"

"No, not enough!"

"One hundred?"

"Still not enough!"

"How much do you have in mind then?"

Slowly bringing forward the fern from behind her back and placing it in Xu Youzhi's lap, she says: "Mr. Xu, what you lost in this land is invaluable; it couldn't be bought back even if you offered to pay a thousand or ten thousand dollars."

Xu Youzhi is astounded by the sophistication of the words coming out of the mouth of this baby-faced girl. Recovering from the initial shock, he admits: "Yes, I had...I had a daughter here."

Now it is Xing Xing's turn to be stunned. She had said what she did because she is smart and she took an educated guess about the emotions of a native returning from abroad. Now that she has unwittingly reopened an old wound in Mr. Xu, she is suddenly at a loss for what to say.

"She would be 42 now."

Xing Xing's beautiful eyes widen with bewilderment at Mr. Xu's words. "What! She would be about Rulan's age then."

To Xing Xing's mind, a woman is already terribly old at forty. Come to think of it, it's been over forty years since Liberation. So of course if Mr. Xu had a daughter then, she would be that age now.

Recovering from her shock, she sits down docilely next to Mr. Xu and asks in a timid voice: "Mr. Xu, have you tried to locate your daughter?"

"Oh, it's a big world, and the trail must have gone cold. Where would I begin to look?"

"Mr. Xu, you should give it a try. Maybe it's written in your stars that you'll be reunited. Hmm, she's 42. That means she has the sign of the ox, and the same age as the People's Republic..."

Counting on her fingers, she looks as if she's ready to start the search right away. Xu Youzhi is amused by this seemingly unfeigned seriousness of purpose. "My child! You are so delightful. I like to see young people enjoying themselves. There are people in mainland China who like to act older than their age, and they walk about with a long face as if everyone owed them money."

"You are so right, Mr. Xu. Rulan is one of them. She rarely utters a word all day long. She's so weird. She is still single and some say she is a pervert." Xu Youzhi's observation has given her an opportunity to ramble on and on.

Mr. Xu admonishes her with a flick on her nose: "Young lady, watch your language!"

Xing Xing blushes. When the subject of sex comes up in conversations with her mentor or among students on campus, it is treated as casually as if one were talking about fashion. She never imagined this man from Taiwan would be so...prudish. She drops her eyes with a blush and changes the subject: "Mr. Xu, do you like cheerful girls?"

"Of course!" Mr. Xu has a booming voice. "No matter how harsh the reality of life gets, we must face it. Make every day a cheerful day as long as you live."

"Will you accept me as your daughter?" She snuggles closer, gazing up at him with a child-like twinkle in her eyes.

Looking up absently, Xu Youzhi sees a squirrel scuffling in the trees. From the far side of the dense woods rises the murmur of the stream flowing down the back of the yellow dragon. It is a distant, unearthly sound that doesn't give a clue as to where the water comes from or where it is going, a sound outside of space and time. Xing Xing's silky-haired head nestled against his chest gives off a pleasant scent of shampoo. He scoops her up into his arms as he would his own little child.

She quickly flings her arms around his neck and whispers in his ear: "Daddy!" He feels her warm breath tickling his ear and is on the point of saying something when an anguished cry suddenly descends from above, sending a shudder through his body, causing him to involuntarily release her.

"Ah—Long—"

Large beads of sweat appear on Xu Youzhi's forehead and his face blanches. "Who is it? Who is bellowing?"

Xing Xing has absolutely no clue.

The plaint echoes back from the surrounding mountains: "Ah—Long—" The despairing, forlorn tone is that of an anguished, death-defying cry escaping from the depth of Hades.

Mr. Xu puts a hand to his chest, his breath quickening and his face distorted with excruciating pain. Xing Xing is thrown into a panic. "What? Mr. Xu! Do you have a heart condition? Do you have heart disease?"

Suddenly remembering the oxygen pouch entrusted to her by her mentor, she takes it out and places it in Mr. Xu's nose, imploring: "Inhale! Inhale!"

But Mr. Xu is already unable to speak; he falls backward and faints.

Shaking with fright, Xing Xing throws down the oxygen pouch and screams: "Help! Help!"

The only response to her cry for help is that desperate call: "Ah—Long—"

The call travels across the miles and miles of snow mountains, leaps over the winding yellow dragon and, traveling through every inch of this life and the next, finally takes the shape of a rope tightening around Xu Youzhi's heart.

8

In the struggle back from the brink of death, the world has turned into a melting candle. The dim, flickering light of the candle reveals a pair of small bead-like black eyes glaring at him—those are the eyes of the Yellow Dragon Immortal in the Huanglong Temple. Although he has not entered the temple, the immortal's cold, impassive eyes stare at him steadily and suggestively.

You advance from the prime of your life toward

old age, struggling with futile thoughts, and before you know it you have come to the end of the road. Nothing is eternal, but fate has arranged everything down to the minutest details, and the Yellow Dragon Immortal has everything and everyone in the palm of his hand.

The racing of his heart is unbearable. Just as forty years ago, when he knocked on that fateful door and it sprang open to reveal the darkness inside...

Back when Mr. Xu was known as Yun Long, it was not actually he nor his friend Gu Long who was put on the blacklist, but Meng Long, the attractive college girl with hair bobbed about her ears.

Meng Long was from a prominent family; her father was a renowned commander of Chinese nationalist party, or KMT, troops tasked with mopping up "bandit troops." At one of their happy family dinners, the daughter stole her father's battle plans and delivered them to the very "bandits" targeted by the expedition. Not long after, those "bandits" conducted an operation that wiped out the KMT troops, numbering in the many thousands, under her father's command.

Meng Long publicly severed all relations with

her family and was sworn into the communist party under a red hammer-and-sickle flag. Straight away she was sent to a college campus with the task of leading the "anti-hunger anti-persecution" student movement.

Yun Long and Gu Long were Meng Long's junior by one year. One had come from an isolated farm village deep inland and the other was the son of a small-time rural landlord. The two freshmen had just been admitted to college and had not yet had time to shed their country boy manners. They knew precious little about Marx or communism, and had no real understanding of the communist party, but they were won over by Meng Long's beauty.

The fact is that Meng Long, who always wore a simple blue cotton cheongsam, was the most plainly dressed among the many female students who flaunted their more colorful outfits. But she stood out with her tall slender figure, oval-shaped face that was naturally pink and white without the aid of makeup, and "phoenix" eyes that slightly slanted up at the outer corners and were coupled with eyebrows arched like graceful willow twigs. She exuded an aura of purity and there was a fearless, indomitable look, bright as sunshine, in her eyes.

To the two callow youths, who were captivated by her, Meng Long was a beautiful statue radiating the colors of a sunny day in early spring. Meng Long was the communist party and the communist party was Meng Long. Whatever task was handed down by Meng Long, they would vie to be the first to carry it out to perfection. While the student movement grew robustly, young love had not been idle either. Meng Long had no lack of suitors, but she had eyes only for these two young dragons.

They went along from freshman year to sophomore and then from sophomore to junior. But of the two, which one was the preferred one? Whom did she love more?

The question tormented Yun Long, but Gu Long was like a brother to him. Neither had the heart to reveal his secret ardor for fear of hurting the other.

One day Meng Long asked for a meeting at the edge of town, far from campus.

In the twilight a soft drizzle was falling. Behind a shabby temple, magpies hopped about near a footpath. On low hills, frail young oleanders swayed in the wind, and towering cypresses, whose dense foliage took on the look of evening clouds, projected an alluring green.

She stepped out of the shelter of a cypress into the pouring rain. She was holding a bright red oilpaper umbrella that gave the impression of a red strawberry.

The scene is etched in his memory, clear as a reflection in still water.

Under the umbrella she exhibited an unusual nervousness, which heightened her color and turned even her earlobes red like tender petals of a peach blossom.

He was infinitely thankful, feeling that the evening rain had finally washed away the mist of uncertainty and had delivered her to him free and clear. He strode toward her, filled with excitement and passion, believing that the questions, the doubts and suspicions, the heroic rhetoric and revolutionary zeal, all were finally going to have their reward. This girl just slightly his senior was going to be his palace, his spotless, splendid little kingdom under the big blue sky.

But then he saw Gu Long hurrying toward them on another path. He realized only then that she had asked both of them to meet her there.

She said to them: "We are in great danger. The KMT reactionaries in their death throes are putting up a fierce fight, and all who have taken part in progressive movements are in danger. Many of our comrades have been evacuated in small groups and I am leaving shortly."

He was intelligent enough to grasp immediately the implications of what she said, but Gu Long was still confused. "Leaving? Where are you going?"

"I'm going to Yan'an!"

"Oh!" Gu Long added immediately: "Then I'll come with you!"

Yun Long had long vowed that he would follow her to the end of the world. He was annoyed that Gu Long had forestalled him and quickly said: "I'll come too."

He hated sounding like a parrot, but she was very pleased. "That's wonderful! We'll meet in Yan'an."

The two dragons gave her a startled look. "What! Aren't we leaving together?"

"Er, it's like this," Meng Long explained in a soft voice. "I have a special situation and it would be risky for you to travel with me. It's best that we leave separately. It's safer."

She appeared somewhat nervous and started to absently twirl the shaft of the umbrella, spinning it faster and faster until the raindrops flew in all directions from the bright red, smooth canopy into the air, into the soft drizzle floating down from the sky.

"The first one of you to reach Yan'an will get to marry me!"

These words tumbled out at a great speed. He could see her dark eyes glitter like gemstones.

When he hurried back to campus to pack a few things for the road, he found Gu Long's bed had already been stripped bare. The darkness of night was tempting like the moist eyes of a young woman, and he set off, abandoning college and the high expectations of his family.

There were checkpoints on the railroad to stop suspicious-looking travelers for interrogation. Despite the risk, he rode the train for a distance, but when inspections became more frequent, he avoided the train and traveled on foot from Jinyang (Mianyang) to Jiangyou, then on to Pingwu, walking upstream along the Fu River.

He didn't know how Gu Long was travelling,

but he was convinced he was smarter than Gu Long and would reach Yan'an first. His blood raced in his veins, like the turbulent flow of the Fu River. A red spinning umbrella in his mind's eyes drew him on.

He hurried along, and even when he slept under the stars at night, he could see and feel the presence of that red umbrella spinning off rain water. Sometimes when he walked in a daze, he felt as if his body was floating under the umbrella. He could almost breathe her fragrance.

One day he got lost.

It was an overcast day. He pored over his map for a long time but could not be sure where he was. Clouds and mists stretched as far as the eye could see. He reckoned that if the Creator had erased Eden from the face of the earth, there was no reason to suppose He would not do the same to a mere mortal lost in the wilderness.

He did not know if the decision to go to Yan'an was the right one. And he wondered how Meng Long was doing. Hemmed in by mountain after mountain shrouded in mist, he thought with despair that if he were given a chance to return to the hustle and bustle of the civilized world, to be able once again to stroll on the campus and read in the soft light of a lamp, he would gladly give up all protest and revolt and return to being a humble ordinary man.

As he walked on, not knowing exactly where he was going, he saw, through the veil of the mist, a giant yellow dragon looming ahead.

"Ah, a dragon!" The sight had the effect of a shot in the arm. Presently his heartbeat quickened and sensation came back to his numbed body.

9

Inside the tour bus, now traveling along at a prudent pace, his tour companions, Xing Xing, Sha Sha, Songlin and Rulan, gather around Mr. Xu, watching solicitously and anxiously over him, calling his name. He looks feebly at them, as if searching for that pair of bead-like black eyes or that giant yellow dragon, and asks: "Who was there?"

"An old man collecting medicinal herbs. We were lucky he came by!" Xing Xing wants to be the first to tell him what had happened: "He saved you with the herbs in his basket. He was admirable!"

"What herbs?"

Remembering just in time that Mr. Xu has an aversion to traditional Chinese herbal medicines, Xing Xing shuts her mouth. But she remembers the chaotic scene: amid her loud wailing and cries for help, a strange-looking old man dressed in black appeared out of nowhere and deftly got some herbs out of his basket, which he chewed before stuffing them into the mouth of the unconscious Mr. Xu. Of course this detail must be kept from Mr. Xu, for if he knew he had ingested herbs mixed with someone else's saliva, he would be so disgusted that he could go into another faint.

"Mr. Xu, oh, Mr. Xu... Oh, no, I should call him daddy now. Daddy, please don't pass out again. God bless you and get well!" Xing Xing silently wishes.

With teardrops perched at the corners of her eyes, Xing Xing, thankful that a disaster has been averted, gazes affectionately at Mr. Xu. The sight warms the heart of Xu Youzhi, who marvels at how simple and natural mainland girls can be. With great fondness he takes Xing Xing's delicate hand into his. "My child, where is that man now?"

"That man...disappeared!" Xing Xing falters.

At the critical moment the man had descended like a *deus ex machina*, and as soon as the patient was out of danger he made a quiet exit. She didn't even realize he'd left. She vaguely recalls that Chen Songlin and the others had by then arrived on the scene. While she clearly remembers it was the man who carried Mr. Xu on his back to the shoulder of the main road, Chen Songlin and the others swear none of them saw that. But for the plain fact that Mr. Xu has survived the near fatal sudden illness, she would be tempted to think that the man was only a figment of her imagination.

"What did that old herb collector look like?" Chen Songlin asks from behind Xing Xing. "How was he dressed?"

With the expression of someone startled out of a dream, Xing Xing quietly withdraws her hand and turns around to describe the man, supplementing the account with gestures: "He wore his hair this long, he had a long beard like this. He was thin and swarthy but his eyes shone. He was dressed in black, and looked like a savage!"

"I see." Chen Songlin looks away and gazes out the window, as if to pierce through the mountains and forests, which are progressively losing their sharp outlines in the failing light.

No longer asking questions, Xu Youzhi leans back in his seat, quietly closing his eyes. Believing that he is resting, the others are careful not to disturb the quiet as the bus continues its winding journey on the mountain road.

It wouldn't occur to the others that Xu Youzhi is at this moment gnawed by regret. He regrets not having gone into the Huanglong Temple to pay homage yet again to the Yellow Dragon Immortal, to find out if the Immortal's beady black eyes held any revelations for him.

10

"Mr. Xu, I've brought your medicines!"

Once the bus had arrived at the Jiuzhaigou Valley Nature Reserve and lodging had been arranged, Xing Xing headed directly to the local medical station, without taking a rest, and obtained a bunch of drugs, including heart medicines and vasodilators, for Mr. Xu.

Half inclined in his bed, with a rolled-up quilt cushioning his back, Xu Youzhi takes the medications from Xing Xing, examining the tablets and capsules closely with narrowed eyes, as if to check their ingredients.

Xing Xing fetches a fresh glass of drinking water. "Mr. Xu, it's time to take your medicine!"

Shaking his head, Xu Youzhi returns the tablets one by one to the containers. "No, I'm not taking them."

"But why?" Xing Xing is very disappointed.

"I'm not taking anything. I am not ill." He acts like a stubborn boy.

Not one to give up easily, Xing Xing picks out a few vitamin tablets and a traditional Shexiang "musk" heart-saving pill, saying: "At least take these."

"No," Xu Youzhi says, giving a light tap to the back of her hand. "I have no faith in medicine made here."

"Why?" Xing Xing can't help asking. "Are you saying our drugs are inferior? Not made to specifications? Not up to recognized standards?"

"No, no, I'm not saying this for any of those reasons. The thing is," he continues after a slight pause, "we have a problem adjusting to them."

Xing Xing is jarred by the inadvertent use of the word "we," which draws a dividing line between two camps—in this case, "we" means Sha Sha and himself, excluding herself, her mentor, and Rulan. This is an unpleasant reality.

But Xing Xing is open-minded. In an instant change of mood, she covers her mouth and starts to giggle. She is tempted to tell him: "You adjust very well. You even swallowed an herbal preparation mixed with saliva. You adjust even better than we do. You are well adapted to a primitive way, a savage land."

Her laughter puzzles Xu Youzhi. "Bad girl! You are up to no good."

Xing Xing keeps on laughing but says nothing. She knows that she must be careful about what she says, because misspoken words could have serious consequences. On the other hand the hearty laughter of a young woman can never go wrong and never fails to enchant.

Still laughing, she begins picking up the scattered tablets. Then she detects an odd, bitter smell on his breath. She instinctively steps back and averts her face. "Are you running a fever?"

"Good girl. You are very observant. But fevers are for young people. Older people don't get them easily."

"You are not old at all." Xing Xing gives him a playful glance of feigned annoyance, and runs her hand over his hair. "Your hair is still very dark."

"Silly child! It's dyed black," he says with a laugh.

"Dyed? It doesn't have a dyed look." Xing Xing has a look of naïve surprise. "I've seen people with dyed hair. It's either all black or has white at the roots. Your hair is salt and pepper. Did you have to dye it strand by strand to get that effect?"

"Yes, this kind of dyeing solution is very expensive," Mr. Xu explains in all seriousness. "It's not available here."

"Oh, don't tell me even a dyeing solution..." She leaves her sentence unfinished and makes a face, sticking out her tongue mischievously. Suddenly, without warning, she bends over him and takes his temperature by pressing her tender, moist, pursed lips against his forehead. "It's so warm! You must be running a fever!"

Then she gives a cheer as if she had just hit a jackpot. She expected Mr. Xu to be pleased, but he merely gives the back of her head a pat. "Get off me now. I never kiss girls."

"Are you saying you don't allow girls to kiss you?" She straightens up pouting, a wronged expression on her face.

"Yes!"

"What about your wife?"

"Not even the wife."

"What an eccentric old man," Xing Xing thinks to herself. Turning around self-consciously she says: "Good night! I'm going back to my room."

"Come here!" Grabbing her delicate hand, Mr. Xu raises it to press against his cheek and gives it a light pat. "Older people have their eccentricities—all right, go now!"

Xing Xing leaves the room, closing the door behind her. It is late. The moon, with only a tiny sliver in shadow, hangs over the highland, bright and full, heartbreakingly beautiful. With a blink of her delicate eyelids, tears well up without warning.

Day 3

Upon the Magic Mirror of the Goddess Semo

1

"Tuesday, May 21..."

This is the line that Rulan enters in her notebook as Xing Xing is still in a deep sleep and Sha Sha busies herself with filtering her drinking water for the day. She vaguely senses that this will be an unusual day.

Outside the window the sonorous voice of Xu Youzhi can be heard, telling everybody to get ready for departure. This is normally Chen Songlin's duty, but today Mr. Xu has forestalled him.

In the early morning light Xu Youzhi appears in high spirits, his sparse hair meticulously combed back, his face clean-shaven, his chin smooth like a peeled boiled egg.

"Mr. Xu, are you sure you are well enough to travel?" Chen Songlin hurries out of his room. "I was going to move the departure time back so that you could rest a while longer."

"Let's be clear." Xu Youzhi looks at him steadily, saying: "Do I or do you need rest?"

"Well, I...I am feeling the weight of my years too." Indeed one would think it was not the executive from Taiwan who was ill yesterday, but this sickly-looking professor from the mainland, unshaven with long and untidy sideburns, dark shadows around eyes that are squinted as if averse to light, and a slight stoop.

"Ha ha ha!" Xu Youzhi bursts into hearty laughter and gives Chen Songlin a slap on the shoulder. "Young man! You try to look older than your years by staying up late, smoking and forgetting to shave. But when you reach my age, looking younger than your years will become your obsession."

With a cryptic sigh, Chen Songlin boards the bus without a word. It's only after the bus has traveled some distance that he finds his voice again and begins to hold forth with self-assurance: "We are leaving Huanglong Ravine, but I believe that our impressions of this place have been stored in our brains. According to the number-axes approach to creative writing..."

To Rulan's ears Chen Songlin's voice sounds somewhat hollow. He may be an eloquent speaker but he does not know what he's talking about. It's almost as if he needed this steady flood of words to cover up something, to prop something up.

She breathes a soft sigh, not without feeling some sympathy for him, for she understands that everyone could at some point find himself at such an awkward pass. Everyone is guilty of engaging in a lot of idle talk during the course of the day. Without idle talk, people would not come together and society as we know it would not exist. Idle talk is not in itself reprehensible; it becomes objectionable when "men of respectability" use profound-sounding idle talk to interpret simple, shallow idle talk, causing an exponential growth of idle talk in society.

"Yesterday Mr. Xu saw in the yellow dragon a symbol of the rise of the Chinese nation. I see a beast imprisoned in a dense fog, the stream and the waterfalls being its torrential tears. So you see, there can be very different ways of writing about the same topic—the dragon. Clearly the material world is infinitely differentiable and 3-D space is amenable to an infinite number of possible angles of observation—an unlimited number of conceptions. When we conceive a work, every one of us has in his head a unique, gigantic information reaction field, whose workings are as mysterious as the riddle of the Sphinx...Xing Xing!"

The seating has been rearranged today. Xing Xing is seated next to Mr. Xu; Rulan keeps Sha Sha company, and Chen Songlin sits by himself. Xing Xing lifts her head, which reaches almost up to Mr. Xu's shoulder, and gazes at her mentor with that familiar look of having just been startled out of her sleep, mumbling: "I...I don't have any particular feeling about the dragon."

"What about you?" Chen Songlin turns to Rulan. "Our woman of letters! You must have an information reaction field that stands out from the rest of us."

"Seriously, I have never liked dragons." Rulan didn't expect the question. "I hate dragons and don't want to use them as a subject for my essay."

"But weren't all of you excited by the sight of the yellow dragon yesterday?"

"This is a riddle worthy of the Sphinx," Rulan says with a straight face. "Come to think of it, a prehistoric reptile with claws such as the dragon is a symbol of all that is outdated and reminds one of rigor mortis, no matter how you look at it. It has no life and no beauty."

"What! What? What is this nonsense?" Xu Youzhi suddenly cries out like an impetuous young man. "What right do you have to wax eloquent about the dragon? Let me tell you, I..."

"We know. Your name is Yun Long, cloud dragon!" Sha Sha adds her penny's worth to the discussion.

With a grunt Xu Youzhi warns her: "Don't interrupt people when they are speaking." Giving Sha Sha a sharp look out of the corner of his eyes, he goes on: "Forty years ago, on my way to Yan'an I passed that way; and when I saw for the first time that giant golden yellow dragon I could hardly believe my eyes. As I advanced in a sort of a daze, the dragon seemed to come alive and looked more powerful and fiercer than ever. One moment it appeared to have flown down from heaven and the next moment it was poised to soar into the sky.

"I stood there stupefied. The clouds and mists were churning and the dragon seemed to be gyrating in some kind of struggle; it vaguely suggested labor pains. All my senses were quickened and I felt I'd turned into a dragon myself. I suddenly felt fortified by an unusual strength and power, and with a roar I broke into a run. As I vaulted over the claws and clambered up the dragon's body I had a sense that I had been possessed by the spirit of a dragon. I believed that up there—across the forehead of the dragon, at the source of the spring of golden living water—must be written the secret code of my destiny. I intended to crack that code!

"By the time I climbed to the summit, night had fallen, and the dragon, the snowy peaks and I all sank into the obscuring darkness.

"At that hour the mountaintop entered a veil of shadows, as if it had been plunged into the darkness of a womb, suddenly deprived of light, of its past and its future. The colorless, amorphous, vast darkness was like a dream of the beginnings of life.

"The wind gusted, nearly knocking me off balance. My sweat-drenched shirt felt like an ice-cold sheet of steel on my back and my stomach growled with hunger. I wanted to turn back but my strength had deserted me. The cold, hunger and strong winds impelled me toward a crumbling temple.

"The light of a candle, visible through a window, got my hopes up. Maybe a charitable old Taoist monk lived in that temple and would be willing to free my soul from the purgatory of the freezing night and ferry me across to a warmer morning. But the small temple nestled near the crest of that lofty mountain had its doors and windows tightly closed, like the lowered brows and dropped eyelids of a chaste, old-fashioned spinster. The door refused to budge despite my pushing.

"Just as I put up my hand to knock on the door, I heard human sounds behind it. I dropped my trembling hand, for what I detected was not the transcendent chanting of sutras but the very worldly sounds of human emotions and desires.

"Why would there be people in such a place? Hopefully they were not bandits fleeing from the law!

"I shivered at the idea and had second thoughts about going in. I was at a loss as to what to do. I wanted to keep warm by stamping my feet but was afraid that might alert the people inside. But once I stood still my already freezing body felt like it had fallen into an ice cave. Staring fixedly at the door, I felt a sudden shudder of fear, but the door seemed to exert a mysterious allure, drawing me on. I was seized with an irresistible urge to push the door open. To me, the door was a mouth, a mouth in that wall, in that temple, a mouth that would lead to the unknown. I was sure a howl would be wrung from that mouth the moment it was opened..."

2

"So, did you knock?" As if listening to a suspenseful tale, Xing Xing asks, her heart in her mouth: "Did you finally knock on that door?"

Lowering his head, Xu Youzhi presses his hand down on its crown. "I have relived that moment countless times but I couldn't figure out what I feared. In those circumstances, frankly, there was nothing to be afraid of, even if those were bandits inside the temple. I was penniless so I had nothing to lose if I ran into robbers. It would have come down to a choice between dying of cold by staying outdoors or sharing the indoor warmth with bandits. The latter looked like a more attractive option."

"Then why..." The suspense proves too much for even Rulan to bear.

"Today I've finally understood what I was thinking when I sat in the empty lot in front of the Huanglong Temple, too weak to go in that temple door. It suddenly struck me that what I had feared then was that howl, that earth-shattering howl I expected would issue from the door and seal my fate!"

"You mean you did go in?" Rulan asks softly, feeling a pang of conscience for having walked away unfeelingly the other day. When you think about it, the rich are no less human than the poor and they need healing ointments on the bruises of their souls just as much.

Nodding, Xu Youzhi continues: "I mustered enough courage to once again put up my hand. With an effort I clenched my hand, which had been frozen stiff, and tapped lightly on the door, which had long lost its painted color and its gloss.

"There was no answer. Thinking I had knocked too softly I knocked again. The voices inside fell silent and my heartbeat quickened. In the hush I got the feeling that behind the door, eyes were watching me in a tense silence. I was not entirely clear about the reason for the tense face-off but felt its thrill. I mustered my strength to pound on the door.

"That produced a fluster of movement in the temple, accompanied by the sounds of busy footsteps and objects knocked over. But the door remained closed. I felt at once angered and elated by this resistance. Apparently, while I may have feared 'ghosts' inside, the 'ghosts' were no less afraid of humans. My self-confidence was given an immense boost by this thought and I braced for a fair fight with whatever might lurk inside.

"I started raining blows on the door, shouting at the top of my voice, 'Open the door! Open the door!'

"And the door opened without warning. It was so unexpected that I fell forward from the momentum of my continued knocking and found myself engulfed by an indescribable warmth. I held my breath, afraid to make a sound lest this dream, built of all the sensations of mind and body, be shattered. Then I heard my name called in a voice filled with delighted surprise. I found my voice and made a cry of my own: 'Meng Long!'"

"Ah, such a beautiful name! It must belong to a young lady. Mr. Xu, I understand now." Xing Xing claps her hands with delight. "This Meng Long must be the girl you loved! So you found her in the temple!"

Chen Songlin is happy too. "It's a very exciting story, Mr. Xu. I have always said that love is a vector; it takes aim, tracks, targets and attacks. Your miraculous reunion proves my theory. Hey, why are you petrified like that?"

"I was petrified like this then." There is deep pain in Xu Youzhi's voice.

Sha Sha titters as she says: "You should have taken her in your arms and kissed her..."

"I did take her into my arms." For once Xu Youzhi has not lost his temper with Sha Sha. "You should know that it was the first time I came into bodily contact with a woman. I admit I did not do a very good job of it, but the feeling—all right, I will spare you the details. I wanted to kiss her, but in the heat of the moment I didn't know where to land that kiss. The moment my fumbling lips found her forehead, she pushed me away."

"Did she no longer love you?" asks Sha Sha.

"No, after she pushed me away she stood

there. Her face was flushed; she was nervous and embarrassed, pained and delighted, bashful and sheepish. Taking heart once again, I said to her in a playfully peremptory tone: 'Meng Long, you can't run away from me. You are going to marry me.'

"But she gestured toward the altar behind her, and covered her face with her hands. Looking up, I saw only the statue of the Yellow Dragon Immortal about a foot tall, staring ahead with his black eyes, an inscrutable expression on his clay face.

"The grim-faced clay statue was depressing, but the joy of reunion brightened everything. It was like grasping a dream! Meng Long was standing right in front of me, in the flesh! When I was going to reach out to her again, I heard a cough, and taking a second look in the direction of the altar, I saw, near the altar in the dim light of a candle, my college classmate and good friend Huang Gu Long, sitting immobile at the foot of the wall!

"I...with a loud wail I ran toward the door. Meng Long rushed up to me and tried to hold me back but I shoved her aside. She threw herself on me again, clasping one of my legs with her arms to prevent me from leaving. I kicked and tried to shake her off. I said

'Let go of me! Let go of me!'"

The vehicle comes to a complete stop. In front of them towers a huge rock with a surface as smooth as a mirror. This is the Baojing Cliff, Magic Mirror Cliff, an entry point to the scenic Jiuzhaigou Valley Nature Reserve.

3

During the spring about ten thousand years ago, Dage, the male mountain god, started his courtship of the female mountain goddess Semo. Dage sang ten thousand love songs to Semo, and every time he sang, the devil Xiemo harassed him. In a rage Dage tackled Xiemo in a fight, defeating him and marrying Semo. But in the heat of combat, a mirror—a token of his love for Semo—was accidentally dropped by Dage and shattered into 108 pieces.

The defeated devil was pinned under the huge rock of the Magic Mirror Cliff. But the mirror was beyond repair and the fragments turned into 108 pools dotting the mountain landscape, giving off an iridescent, breathtaking beauty for eternity.

The essence of Jiuzhaigou is its water: water surrounding the mountains; water at the foot of hills; water flowing through forests; water skipping over rocks; water roaring down sheer cliff faces; water cascading, rushing out of deep dales; water reflecting the azure sky and white clouds, green trees and red flowers; water making music, water roaring down rapids. Water—Dage's semen, life's melody, nourishing Semo for ten thousand long years, nourishing her into a beauty of a thousand charms.

The group sets out from the Magic Mirror Cliff. As they enter the Shuzheng Gully, one of the three main gullies forming an antler-like trifurcation in Jiuzhaigou, they see all around them swift-flowing clear streams. Pines, cypresses and willows stand gracefully in the water, and through the lush foliage waft the crisp chirps of birds. The abundant clumps of green grass in the stream sway with the flow of the water. They look like countless sparkling emerald trays holding up the luxuriant masses of tall ancient trees along the banks.

There is a simple elegance in the primitive landscape and an ethereal beauty in the wilderness. The travelers almost feel they have found paradise on earth. They savor this thrill of body and mind in spellbound silence.

But Sha Sha still can't get that unfinished story out of her mind, asking: "Mr. Xu, did you or did you not leave the temple that night?"

"Are you joking? Where could I go in that freezing night?" The stern and forbidding expression on Xu Youzhi's face does not faze Sha Sha. And only Sha Sha has the temerity to press on with the question: "Then you stayed?"

Xu Youzhi's face darkens as he hurries off in giant strides.

Sha Sha's enthusiasm is undiminished. "Wow, how wonderful! To know what happens next...Ah, Professor Chen, rotate your Rubik's Cube, quick!"

Rulan glances over her shoulder at Chen Songlin, who smiles but says nothing. Xing Xing, however, is quick with a quip: "The Rubik's Cube of creative writing has stopped turning!"

Sha Sha retorts: "How can it stop working? I know what happened next: the two men confronted each other with hostility in their eyes. They glared at each other for...all of five minutes, then there was a slight movement. One of them suddenly raised a fist and the other let fly with a kick. The two dragons came to blows, they were locked in a battle to the death just like Xue Baoding's two suitors fighting for her love."

Sha Sha's story-telling, accompanied by gestures, prompts Xing Xing to observe in an undertone: "Third-rate martial art flick made in Hong Kong or Taiwan!"

Rulan, however, finds it interesting. "Sha Sha, which dragon, would you say, won the fight?"

"Oh, well..." Casting a glance in the direction of Xu Youzhi, who is walking at the head of the group, Sha Sha whispers into Rulan's ear: "Of course it had to be our Yun Long...No, no, if he had won, how come he didn't marry that Miss Meng Long? I know, he must have lost to Gu Long. Then he probably left in a huff for Taiwan. Hee hee!"

Rulan puts a hand over her mouth to smother a chuckle. They did not reckon on the sensitive hearing of Xu Youzhi, who stops short and looks over his shoulder. Rulan, startled and fully expecting him to blow his top, hastens to swallow her chuckle, only to see him roll up a sleeve, revealing an arm smooth and strong as that of a man in his prime. "Look, all of you, take a look!"

The group throngs around him to find out what he means. Xu Youzhi flexes his muscles at Chen Songlin. "Going back forty years, no one would be my match!"

Amused and playing along, Chen Songlin backs away from him. "I'm not your match even now!"

Sha Sha twirls and spins with delight: "Ah, I see, I see—our dragon won the fight! Hats off—hats off to our hero!" But Xu Youzhi, lowering his arm, says with a twitch of his mouth in a parody of a smile: "Are you kidding? How could I have stayed in that place and got into a fight? Truth is I wouldn't have stayed in there if my life had depended on it, if it had otherwise meant freezing to death."

With that he starts off at a brisk pace, even hopping over a ditch cutting across the way, although there is a hint of unsteadiness in the brisk gait adopted by an old man looking to impress. As Rulan debates in her mind whether to catch up and give him a hand, Xing Xing has already pre-empted her. Helping to steady him, Xing Xing asks: "Mr. Xu, where are we now?"

"We are at Reed Lake!"

A long, narrow lake is sandwiched between two

dense rows of reeds extending for miles. The water in the lake is so clear you can see its bottom; the aquatic weeds sway with the currents and fish swim back and forth. Xing Xing picks up a stone and throws it in the lake. The stone, as if it had a life of its own, glints brightly as it sinks in a slow swaying motion toward the bottom of the cold, blue lake, its silence unperturbed.

With the morning fog lifted, the blue surface of the lake appears bright and cheery in the sun. Even the water particles thrown into the air by the waves are suffused with a mellow glow. Only a few steps away, the water surprisingly changes its color. Blue gives way to purple, and when a light breeze wrinkles the lake, it's as if beautiful violet blossoms suddenly break out across its surface. The group's members pause in their walk and turn in a slightly different direction only to find that, in the shadow of the reeds, the purple and deep blue have turned into the tender green of new leaves. It is a changeable green: at one moment it is emerald, at another, the color of jade or the somber gleam of an elegant cat's eye.

There appears in Xu Youzhi's eyes a glimmer of transparent moisture. And for some reason hot tears suddenly roll down Rulan's cheeks. Sha Sha asks in astonishment: "What's the matter?"

Rulan smiles through her tears. "It's so beautiful! It reminds me of Monet."

"Ah, you girls of the mainland are so family-oriented!" Sha Sha puts an arm around Rulan. "You think of your mommy even here! I...I would only think of my boyfriend, if at all."

"Sha Sha, you misheard." Rulan gives her arm a pat. "I don't have a mommy. I said Monet. He was a French Impressionist painter. He created miracles of light and color. It's such a pity that he couldn't visit Jiuzhaigou with us."

"Oh, I understand. You were referring to that old Frenchman from the eighteenth century," Sha Sha says.

"The nineteenth century."

"You've always liked him?"

"I can't say I've always liked him." Rulan considers this before saying, "But at this very moment I suddenly feel I love him."

"Oh boy, I'm so jealous!" Chen Songlin interjects. "There are so many outstanding, talented people across China to love, but you prefer to give

your love to an old foreigner from another century!
Am I right, Mr. Xu?"

Xu Youzhi nods gravely. "Hmm, but that century
had its moment of glory, and that old man was young
once."

Rulan says, unable to smother a chuckle: "Mr. Xu,
you are, you are quite..." She feels that this executive
from Taiwan is rather a likable character, and there is
something in him she can relate to, although she can't
quite put her finger on exactly what it is.

"I have no love for Westerners," Xu Youzhi says
unsmilingly. "As for miracles of light and color, there
are no greater miracles than the creations of Nature.
Look, the proof is all around us!"

4

Looking down from the woods, Rulan and the others
cannot help bursting out with a collective "wow" in
the annoying manner of Sha Sha. Tens of thousands
of golden flames—some small like tea cups, others the
size of bowls—leap off the dark blue surface of a lake,
shimmering, dancing and sparkling, brimming with

the brilliant charm of the sun and the glowing smile of the mountain goddess.

"This is the Sparkling Lake," announces Xu Youzhi matter-of-factly. "It is a miracle wrought by the blazing light of the sun."

When the others scramble to take pictures and can't seem to tear themselves away from the spot, Xu Youzhi begins to lose his patience.

"Hurry up! There are more spectacular sights waiting for us—the Five Flowers Lake, for one. It's a canvas of green and yellow, colorful as a peacock's fully deployed fantail. When the lake catches the sun at the deeper spots, golden aureoles form on the teal surface, and when a breeze rises, it sets off iridescent ripples across the water—capturing it is a challenge for the best of painters."

In high spirits, the group sets off again and soon reaches the Pearls Shallows.

At the Pearls Shallows a stream flows down a gentle incline, sending up sprays of sparkling water, reminding one of thousands of pearls bouncing down the slope or an endless stream of dancing notes in an ageless musical composition.

The water is quite shallow here, the bottom

covered with enticingly soft yellow moss. But the travelers, deterred by the coldness of the water, forgo the pleasure of fording the stream barefooted and instead opt for a trestle bridge, which zigzags snakelike toward the densely wooded area.

The wooden bridge takes them into a deep dale, where a waterfall flows down from a cliff. It is like a huge new moon, throwing off bright flashes of light, its roar deafening like a giant's bellow.

Their awe soon gives way to a sense that the bright flashes, like sharp swords, must pierce even staid hearts, stirring a thrill in front of such power and strength. The tall ancient trees, too, struggle amid the deafening roar, straining to break free of the shackles of their roots.

An indescribable excitement swells Rulan's heart, as the rhythm of the roaring sound seems to pulsate in step with her heartbeat. The powerful pounding of the water appears bent on catapulting her from the past into the future.

She feels a sudden dizziness, a craving for support and for a strong shoulder. Steadying herself she sees Xing Xing with her arm through Mr. Xu's—more accurately it is Mr. Xu who puts his arm through

Xing Xing's with the latter leaning on him. Mr. Xu's strong, muscular back inspires a sense of security and reassurance.

A few steps behind, Chen Songlin, in jeans, hands in his pockets and face half buried in the turned-up collar of his coat, appears preoccupied. Sha Sha, close on the heels of Rulan, looks pale, saying: "I feel a little chilly."

"You must be hungry now." Rulan fishes a bag of cookies out of her backpack. "Hey, can we stop here for a rest?"

This brings Chen Songlin out of his reverie: "Yes, sure, let's have some free time." He sits down on the dead trunk of a fallen tree and holds out his hand, with the palm up, toward Rulan. "What kind of snacks do you have there? Sweet or salty?"

Rulan passes the cookies to him and Xing Xing brings out an unopened bag of Taiwanese snacks, spicy dried pork slices, along with some canned drinks. The travelers, whose stomachs grumble with hunger, fall silent as they fumble with the different packaging materials of diverse colors that are thwarting the sating of their hunger. Sha Sha, the only one to forgo food and drink, wanders off toward a trail leading into the woods. Sensing that something is amiss, Rulan grabs a few cookies and sets off after her, all the while munching on the snacks.

The dense leaves over the trail and the dank mist suffusing the woods block natural light, dimming the bright colors of the flowers. Deeper into the woods they have a sense they are groping along in an abyss, but presently the vista opens up: a lake of turquoise water ruffled by a breeze greets their eyes.

Like all lakes in the Jiuzhaigou Valley Nature Reserve, this blue lake is ringed by grassy banks carpeted by wild flowers of all descriptions and colors as well an unfamiliar fern drooping with fat scarlet tassels. A few white swans swim in the lake, their graceful profiles beautifully reflected in the water, the flapping of wings punctuating the quiet air.

Sha Sha gazes off at the lake, not making a sound. Rulan, loath to disturb this magic spell, leans quietly on a tree. Then the stillness of the water is suddenly shattered by a splashing sound, as if someone is swimming. The uncertainty disappears when several little boys emerge, splashing and sloshing out of the blue water like sea monsters.

The boys range in age from five to early teens.

Wet and naked, they dart about like mudfish and splash water on one another. Rulan is wide-eyed with surprise: she doesn't feel warm enough even with a wool sweater on and yet these naked little boys don't seem to mind the cold at all!

"Ah Loong! Ah Loong!" Sha Sha springs to her feet all of a sudden and chases after a boy who has just clambered out of the water. The boy, with a round face, big eyes and a dark complexion, bounds away like a gazelle upon hearing Sha Sha's calls. Sha Sha sets off in hot pursuit and just when she's at the point of catching up with him, the boy dives into the lake. It's some time before he resurfaces, shaking his head like a duckling to get the water off his face. Sha Sha stamps her feet in frustration. "Ah Loong! Come up out of there! Come!"

Worried by Sha Sha's increasingly strange manner, Rulan tries to stop her: "That's enough! Let's go back."

But Sha Sha insists in her Taiwanese accent: "No, I must find my Ah Loong."

"Ah Long?" The name sounds vaguely familiar to Rulan. "That boy is called Ah Long? Do you know him?"

"Goodness! Have you forgotten already?" Sha Sha exclaims. "He is the little shepherd who saved our lives the day of the rain storm. You've forgotten!"

These words of Sha Sha's hit Rulan like a sharp rebuke. She thinks: "Oh how forgetful you are! You are selfish and hypocritical! You nearly forgot that kid who risked his life to snatch you all from the jaws of death!"

But in what circumstance did the little shepherd disappear? And how has he resurfaced here? She doesn't know. Taking another look at the boy, she is no longer so sure about the resemblance. She asks Sha Sha: "Are you sure it's him? Did you take a good look?"

"Of course! I would recognize him if he were reduced to ashes!" Sha Sha is adamant, but then she gives chase to another boy—also a swarthy naked child with a broad forehead and a snub nose, who appears to bear an even greater resemblance to the little shepherd, if only a bit shorter.

When he sees Sha Sha come after him, this boy also runs off laughing, and, instead of diving into the lake, plays hide and seek with Sha Sha, darting about on the lake shore to avoid capture. Sha Sha shouts:

"Rulan, cut him off!"

Rulan hesitates but curiosity gets the better of her and she decides to help Sha Sha intercept the boy—and it doesn't take long to catch hold of him. But before she can make out what he really looks like, the boy, thrashing and wriggling, has already slipped out of her hold.

She straightens up and is recovering from the confusion when she hears sloshing. The boy who dove into the lake has come out of the water and now stands there dripping with water. He plucks a bright red spike from a clump of grass and grinds it between his hands as he looks at her snickering. Sha Sha shouts from a distance: "Hey, it's him, it's him! Don't let him get away!" Rulan looks left and right and seems to see a resemblance in every face, but this resemblance disappears on closer scrutiny. Confused, she senses a deep mystery associated with these naked bodies floating in front of her eyes. Could they be not boys but nymphs, dryads of the forests or naiads of the sea? Or the soul of that missing little shepherd?

Thinking back on the bodily contact she had with the boy, she recalls that the soft and smooth skin had a very peculiar quality to it—as if what she touched was not a human body, not even a physical presence, but a flash of light, a shadow.

"Sha Sha, let's give up. Let's go back!" There is urgency in her voice, for she feels that if she were to stay a moment longer she would go mad.

But Sha Sha stubbornly refuses to go back and chases the kids around as if she were possessed, calling all the while: "Ah Loong, my Ah Loong!"

Rulan is increasingly unsettled by the strangeness of Sha Sha's behavior, and after a few hurried words to Sha Sha, she runs back to where they had their picnic. "Chen...Songlin, come with me! Quickly!" She has forgotten about etiquette and honorific titles in her haste. Chen Songlin springs to his feet, instantly sensing a problem. "What happened? Did Sha Sha disappear again?"

"No," Rulan gesticulates with her hand, continuing, "Sha Sha is chasing a Tibetan boy by a lake over that way."

"Oh," Chen Songlin's face relaxes with relief, "maybe she's just playing, right?" Realizing that the whole thing may not be that serious, Rulan starts to recount with patience what took place: "She was pursuing that kid, claiming he was her Ah Long..."

"What, Ah Long? She is nuts!" Xu Youzhi gets all worked up. "Tell her to come back immediately!"

"I tried, but she refused to come back," Rulan says with a wry expression.

"Then I will fetch her!" Xu Youzhi gets to his feet, grim-faced. "This is intolerable!"

Chen Songlin is quick to dissuade him: "Mr. Xu, you stay here. I'll go."

But Xu Youzhi ignores him and starts off in a huff toward the lake. "I will sack her after this trip…"

Before his words die on his lips a cry is heard: "Ah—Long—"

The group is seized by a familiar terror; everyone is stupefied. Xu Youzhi's face turns ashen, and he murmurs: "What's happening? What's happening?"

Having learned from previous experience, Xing Xing rushes to hold him up and starts to say something when they hear the cry again: "Ah Long—Ah Long—" The voice, with greater hoarseness and despair in it than before, sounds eerily like the last howl of a dying old wolf bidding a final farewell to life.

"Ah, I recognize the voice. It's Gu Long, Gu Long. It's Gu Long calling out to me!" Xu Youzhi gives Xing Xing a push. "Go, quickly! Run after him!"

His body starts to sway and as his mind wanders, he sees young Gu Long lying before the altar of the Yellow Dragon Immortal...

5

That night he stayed in the Huanglong Temple after all.

He had agreed to stay only because of Meng Long's teary entreaties. He had never seen her cry and was confused. He lay down against the wall on the other side of the altar.

At first he felt total despair. He was an obscure speck of dust in the universe. He was an unwanted dog curled up in a corner of the small Huanglong Temple. Naturally he could not fall asleep. Sleep was impossible.

He closed his eyes and covered his ears, wishing that he would fall to his death in the abyss of darkness. But he was agitated by a strange, grotesque force in his chest. Like a mental patient suffering from auditory hallucinations, he felt he could tip over the edge at the sound of a pin falling.

His eyelids no longer functioned properly—although lowered, they quivered with tense, uneasy spasms. They were no longer able to fully close in order to carve out a quiet, dark corner that would afford temporary asylum. Instead, they had become diaphanous membranes, glittering reflectors that sent back to him stark, perpetual daylight.

Everything was projected onto this bright screen.

He heard a soft rustle, which to his ears sounded like the rubbing of cotton clothes. He saw a blue of such splendor, of such softness, and of infinite tenderness.

A cheongsam made from crude indanthrene-dyed cloth hugged her slender, curvaceous form, clinging to her delicate, smooth skin transparent as water.

Ah, water!

Meandering water; sinuous, graceful water; light and lively water; carefree water; water splashing; water rippling...

Gu Long was draped in a silly-looking long black gown, the crude cloth outlining a stiff, rigid form, like a stone, like a tree stump.

But he had that nubile beauty in his arms!

Maybe it was Gu Long that Meng Long loved after all. From the female perspective everything might be turned upside down. And all this time he had been misled by a false impression and had been pursuing a false hope.

In a daze, he saw himself turned into an explosive, black coal, with a fuse lying on the ground like a pigtail of the imperial Qing period.

But the fuse was out of reach and, hard as he strained, he couldn't light it to blow himself up. He woke up with a start, drenched in sweat. Then he heard a slight rustling sound, which was amplified in his eardrum. What sound was it? It sounded different from what he'd heard before.

He had miraculously regained his customary alertness. After a quick analysis he believed he was hearing blouse buttons being undone, hence the rustling. Gu Long's fingers were undoing the blue frog buttons one by one, revealing the snow white peaks, the proud snow white peaks hidden beneath the blue mist, so pure and pristine.

He felt faint. Hoping against hope, he crawled with a great effort toward those snow white peaks.

But there was peak after peak, each more pure

and pristine, and more splendidly curved. He would never reach his destination. He was merely living in a dream.

The long, endless climb exhausted his energy and his courage; he fought for his breath, panting. Then he heard a different kind of panting—subdued female gasps mixed with heavy breathing. A powerful sense that there was something equivocal and dubious going on assailed him, exploding like a thunderclap in his chest.

He finally realized he hadn't blown Gu Long up; instead he had blown himself into smithereens. He surveyed with a malicious pleasure those fragments that flew up and rained down again like flowers thrown by a goddess. He was tempted to laugh out loud: "You are a sad sack of stinking flesh and bone! You are totally useless!"

The disembodied spirit expanded with a vengeance, and soared with the roar of a dragon, a dragon of desire, of great thirst, thrashing and leaping, in pursuit of a sun in a wild canyon.

That sun's primitive blaze started its journey in the ancient times of Houyi, the legendary hero who shot down nine suns. It looked now like a huge incandescent wheel, now a fully ripened sweet cherry. It fired up the dragon, teasing it, sending it into a flying rage, never allowing it a moment of peace.

It was a kind of temptation, a game that had no beginning and no end.

A flow of desire coursed through his veins, but what was killing him was that he had no way of knowing what they were up to. He didn't know. Imagine that he didn't know! Knowledge was a tempting pit of quicksand overgrown with green grass. A witch sat in the pit, flexing the secret dark suction cups on her tentacles and emitting a fatally attractive scent.

He quietly got to his feet and tiptoed past the altar, stealthily approaching the other wall.

He was no longer a dragon but a humble mudfish—an earth-burrowing mudfish.

It's hard to say if he was aware of this. His entire subconscious being fell prey to the power of the suction cups on those tentacles.

The moonlight floated in the air, insinuating its way into the smallest window and the tiniest crack. Its dim light revealed the secret hidden within that quicksand pit: she lay beside him, in the curve of his arm with her head resting on his shoulder. Her soft pretty face was nestled against his chest while his slightly parted lips were kissing her forehead. As his eyes moved down, under the cotton quilt he saw movements whose meaning was unclear to him, and he could make out the vague contours of entwined legs and bodies welded together.

She appeared to have fallen asleep, and his eyelids were heavy with drowsiness. Neither of them was aware of being watched. They were serene and relaxed, like newborn babies. There was a dreaminess in the half light.

The sudden understanding was like a cry from the depth of one's soul, shocking him and knocking the wind out of him. His legs trembled. The two people in each other's arms were unified in an arc, a spiral pattern of the cosmos.

If he were excluded from it, why should the universe exist at all?

Trembling, he took a small step and bent down with the intention of yanking off the quilt and strangling them like baby chickens.

But at that exact moment he had a queer sensation in his back. It was that very special feeling that someone is watching you. He jerked his head around and saw in the dim light that the Yellow Dragon Immortal was gazing at him with a cold glint in his small eyes.

Instantly losing his nerve, he backed away, and in doing so knocked something over with a bang. The loud racket caused a tingling in his scalp. His heart was still thumping wildly after he had returned to where he had been lying down.

Meng Long, probably awakened by the noise, mumbled a question. He bit his lip to prevent himself from making a sound and pretended he was fast asleep.

Then there was a movement on the other side of the altar. He heard hushed words and had the feeling that they were getting up to do something. Strangely enough at this moment he could no longer make out what they were saying or imagine what they were doing. Presently he could hear footsteps clearly coming his way. He believed it was Meng Long.

Meng Long was coming toward him. Why? What did she want?

He had no idea. He was now numb in body and mind. At that moment all his thoughts and desires were crowded out by her light, tender and timid footfalls.

She came to a halt in front of his recumbent form.

He held his breath and kept his eyes tightly shut. She looked at him and gave a soft sigh, bending at the same time to cover him with an extra blanket she brought for the purpose.

The edge of the blanket came up against his chin and he could smell her body scent, mixed with other odors. Unthinkingly he kicked off the blanket, sprang to his feet and grabbed her wrist.

He caught her as she stumbled and, with a heave, picked her up in his arms and strode toward the door.

She was light as a reed and frail as a lamb in his arms. After a brief moment, she began to struggle weakly. "Yun Long! Yun Long! Where are you going?"

"To kill myself!"

He pushed the door open and ran into the wilderness, carrying her.

The first streak of dawn was visible behind the distant mountains. Snow-capped peaks stood tall against the fading night sky. As the wind rose and clouds chased one another across the sky, the first rays of dawn erupted from the mountains. They showered the ground at his feet with shifting streaks of light. Roads appeared everywhere and roads were nowhere to be found. Carrying her he ran aimlessly, unsure where he was heading.

Looking up he saw the yellow dragon again, now blurry and faded, its head held as high as ever in the pale gray light. It was swimming toward that ultimate destination—the universe that looked so attainable.

6

The sudden onset of Xu Youzhi's illness has thrown the group into disarray. Luckily Xing Xing had the presence of mind last night to keep those medicines she had gotten from the local infirmary even though Mr. Xu had told her to get rid of them. She now has them with her: pills to regulate and protect the heart, nitroglycerin tablets and others. She hurriedly pours out the entire contents of the medicine chest and, picking out some of the pills, she stuffs them into his mouth. Right away these medicines made in mainland

China begin to work wonders inside the body of the executive from Taiwan: his heart has readjusted and resumed its normal beat.

The patient is finally out of danger. It's only now the group remembers that Sha Sha is still missing!

Rulan and Songlin search around the lake without finding Sha Sha. Those boys that frolicked in the lake are nowhere to be seen either. They spot a leisurely elderly man in official garb who is waiting patiently for fish to take the bait at the end of his line.

Songlin goes up to him, and prefaces what he's going to say with *Lao xian sheng*, which although it literally means "old gentleman" is the standard polite term for addressing an older man. However the man does not even look up, seeming not to have heard him. A little embarrassed to ask the question he has in mind, he repeats: "*Lao xian sheng.*" But the old man still doesn't look up. Without quite realizing it, Songlin mutters: "I've come to a deaf one. Rotten luck!" He says it so softly that even Rulan has not heard him, but the old man hears it loud and clear. "Young man! You seem to enjoy insulting people."

Rulan hastens to apologize for Songlin. "Sorry, *Lao ren jia*," she says, using another polite term of address. "A friend of ours has gone missing. We are anxious to find her. We are sorry we've offended you."

With a grunt the old man says: "I've no quarrel with your search for a missing friend, but you shouldn't insist on calling me 'old gentleman.' It grates on my ears."

"Old...sorry, what should we call you?" For Sha Sha's sake, Chen Songlin decides to swallow his pride and show the utmost patience with the man.

"What's wrong with calling me comrade?" retorts the old man.

"Old...comrade, may I ask if you saw a young miss—no, no, I mean a young lady?" Chen Songlin asks.

"She is a little plumper than I," Rulan adds, "and she has her hair cut very short."

The old man, finally placated, looks up for the first time at the two and says in earnest: "There was this woman who was wandering about. She wore red lipstick. She doesn't look old but those pants she wore must be from the imperial Qing period. I saw my grandmother wearing them when I was little. They were made with black silk and the trouser legs were so big you could hide two old hens in them. When she walked the pants flapped in the breeze. I don't know if she is the person you are looking for."

This has confused Chen Songlin in no small measure. "Sha Sha always keeps up with the latest fashion. How can she be wearing pants of the imperial Qing style? No, no, it cannot be her."

Rulan says with a chuckle: "It's her. He has just given an exact description of Sha Sha." Not wanting to waste time explaining to Songlin, she asks the old man again: "Old comrade, which way did the young woman go?"

The "old comrade" gestures at the vast forest and the miles and miles of mountains: "She went that way."

Rulan gives a violent start: "Ah, isn't that a virgin forest?"

"Some say that road leads to the Zharu Horse Trail." But the old man is not too sure about it.

"Now what is the Zharu Horse Trail?" It doesn't ring a bell to Rulan, who is clueless about geography. But Songlin nods knowingly. "The Zharu Horse Trail is a narrow track used in the past by caravans of merchants on horseback. It goes across the mountains to the south and is a shortcut to Huanglong Ravine.

Could Sha Sha be heading to Huanglong Ravine?"

At these words, Rulan seems to have an epiphany. "Yes, you are right! She is heading back to Huanglong Ravine. She must have gone back toward Huanglong Ravine!"

"But why would she?" Chen Songlin is no longer so sure. To make a decision he must have a more rational basis.

"I don't know why," Rulan says, "but I have a gut feeling."

"Is it because of that mysterious call in the air?" asks Chen Songlin suddenly.

"Maybe." Rulan hesitates before saying, "If she had only been chasing after those boys, she would be nearby and we would have found her already."

"That call we heard was really eerie." Chen Songlin furrows his brow. "We heard it three times already, even I...but what does it have to do with Sha Sha?"

"What does it have to do with Mr. Xu then? He said it was Gu Long calling him," Rulan retorts.

"It's a whole different story with Mr. Xu," Chen Songlin says in a calm voice. "We have come to know something about his past. He obviously has close bonds with this land; even his fantasies may have some factual basis. But Sha Sha, given her age, is undoubtedly visiting the mainland for the first time. How can she have lost her mind because of that strange call?"

"That cry seems to possess a power to shake people to the depths of their souls." Rulan remembers the unexpected encounter by the swift-flowing Fu River, that savage who appeared on the cliff. "I would even say that none of us has the ability to resist that force."

"You..." Chen Songlin nods his head after gazing at Rulan's face for a long moment. "You may be right. All the mythologies of the world have asserted the immortality of the soul. Even the philosophers have tried to prove it. It appears that for all the upheavals and changes in our societies and the advances in science and technology, mankind will always have a shared soul that will be passed on from generation to generation! Sorry for using language that might sound overly feminine."

"What's wrong with talking like a woman?" Rulan, suddenly angered, shoots back: "Women have a natural affinity with the soul, while men on the other hand have a congenital tendency to betray the soul in their pursuit of fame and status."

"Suppose I am a pursuer of fame and status. I'm asking you now to come with me to find and bring back a betrayed soul and find a home for it. Will you refuse me?" Chen Songlin is quite serious about it.

Rulan is confused: "I'm sorry, but I don't get... your humor, because I've never been...very worldly."

"Same here," Chen Songlin says with a tolerant smile. "We belong to a parochial nation with a poor sense of humor. That's why our soul is so weighed down."

Time doesn't allow them to continue their debate about the soul. After making arrangements for Xing Xing to accompany Mr. Xu to a nearby guesthouse for the night and travel on with him by car to Songfan the next morning, Chen Songlin and Rulan set out along the Zharu Horse Trail to find Sha Sha.

7

"I never imagined there could be places like this in the world. It is at once paradise and—hell." She is fighting for breath and has a splitting headache as she says this.

"Come." He holds out his hand to her. They are trekking across a high mountain and have a hard time adjusting to the thin air.

They feel so close to the sky; the setting sun hangs low like a huge golden goblet overflowing with red wine, radiating a full-bodied, aromatic and cool elegance. Intoxicated, the sky exhibits a hazy moistness, and the snow peaks, also inebriated, are ablaze with splendor. Even the patches of wild dandelions, carpeting the slopes denuded by irresponsible logging, are drunk on the last rays of the setting sun. The afterglow fuzzes the outlines of the leaves and dissolves the shapes of the flowers. All mass and distance, all things humble and lowly have been purified into delicate, fine molecules. Everything is light, rarefied light, the glory before the plunge into darkness. It leaves its traces even in the shadows.

"Ah, lily pads! Monet's lily pads!" Despite suffering from altitude sickness, Rulan dashes in wild elation.

Songlin stays behind, knowing this is not a place where you can find lily pads, but he hates to dampen her high spirits. He has never met another woman who can be so aloof and yet so passionate at the same time, so haughty and yet so lacking in self-esteem. Her reclusive and withdrawn nature and her occasional bursts of naiveté form a huge contrast with the wit, talent and ardent passion characterizing her writing.

This contrast adds to the mystery surrounding her. Nobody knows much about her. She appears to pointedly distance herself from modernity and from life. She appears to be free from wants and desires and she is uninterested in fame or gain. Her beauty, clear as water, is a far cry from the frail, coquettish prettiness of girls. She does not try to hide her wrinkles with makeup. Yet she has somehow managed to maintain the figure of a young girl. In the wash of the last rays of daylight in those high mountains, she is a light blue ghost image created by the orange red of the setting sun.

It suddenly occurs to him that there is little difference between the setting sun and the rising sun. As a metaphor for human youth, it produces the same burning heat, the same release of energy, the same colors and the same brilliance—what comes after, a long day for the one and a long night for the other, is irrelevant.

"Look," she says, walking toward him while holding out a light yellow lotus-shaped flower. The flower is mounted at the end of a thin, tube-like stem with no leaves or thorns.

She has been rendered breathless by the lack of oxygen and is therefore unable to utter more words in praise of the flower. He holds out a hand to her again. Hand in hand they set out, descending from the summit of glory. The denuded hillsides, dotted with dark green sandthorn bushes, remain in the light at this hour. The setting sun, hurried on by the waiting night, splashes the firmament with bands of mauve clouds reminiscent of curtains about to be raised for the performance of a tragedy.

"That flower you picked was a snow lotus," he explains to her. "The snow lotus in the mountains is a symbol of so-called pure love."

"Why so-called?" There is an unusual mischievous wink in her eyes. "Do you mean there is no pure love?"

"Do you think there is?" he turns the question back to her.

Dejected, she says: "Maybe you are right…"

"I'm very disappointed!" He suddenly seizes

her hand, as if in anger, questioning: "Why didn't you contradict me? Why didn't you? You wrote so many love stories! Many people believe you know everything about love!"

No hint of provocation is discernible in his tone, but he seems determined to tear away that veil of mystery. She stumbles with the force of his pull but is not a bit upset. She looks up at him, her face glowing. "Really? My stories were successful? I know everything?"

She suddenly finds herself unable to continue. In the residual light of the dusk, she sees in his eyes a charm that melts her heart. He is not tall nor is he sturdily built; he is even on the thin, frail side, a far cry from what is fashionably considered masculine. If he put on a starched white shirt with a stiff collar and a well-tailored suit, he would look the part of an elegant gentleman. But for some reason he has shown unusual neglect for his personal appearance on this trip, with long strands of unruly hair flopping over his forehead, his temples visibly graying and a button missing from his jacket. He doesn't look like an acclaimed scholar at all but rather has the appearance of an obscure, down-on-his-luck artist.

But it is precisely his hangdog look, his emaciated, pale face topped by rumpled hair, and his labored breathing combined with the strength in his hand, that have created an air of tragedy and deep suffering about him. She experiences a momentary breathlessness. As she watches his eyes, she feels she's drawn unaccountably into a new emotion.

"Let's be on our way," he says to her. "We will be at our destination once we've made it across this mountain."

They shiver in the cold, thin air. Surrounded by a landscape evocative of paradise, their bodies are put through hellish torments. It is these torments that put you in touch with reality, a living reality, instead of a reality of dreams.

8

But in the river of time it is often dreams that come closest to reality.

Xing Xing is not the one and only in Chen Songlin's life. As far as he is concerned, Xing Xing and other girls have brought, with the sunshine of their youth, bright colors into his life, but the flip side of bright light is the dark shadow that invariably accompanies it.

That dark shadow is his dream.

All girls are flowers, but no flower can compare to a budding flower that falls off prematurely. A memory haunts him; if she had lived she would be a menopausal woman now, but an early death has preserved her in the bloom of her youth, making her forever fresh and fragrant.

And so he loves the girls and dotes on them; he likes the tenderness of their bodies and appreciates the quickness of their minds. But he could as little find a way to their hearts as they could his.

There was a female graduate student before Xing Xing, who fell head over heels in love with him. He was on the point of making a life-changing decision on account of her. Then a week into a business trip to Shenzhen he himself had arranged for her, she decided to leave him for a foreign executive.

For them, his charisma, the breadth and depth of his knowledge, his stature and an age that affords a sense of security make up the attraction of a mature man. But the attraction is skin-deep; it has a utopian quality to it. No girl can hope to get the things they want most from life by pursuing utopia. The more important question is whether one possesses enough money to satisfy them. Unless knowledge bears pecuniary fruit, what value does knowledge have?

He has been through much suffering and witnessed many betrayals, including his own. And this means he can no longer experience life in a pure and spontaneous way as before. No one knows how much angst is hidden deep inside of him. Driven by a premonition of growing old and frail, he plows ahead, not daring to rest even for a minute.

"Let's walk faster," he says to Rulan. "We must find lodging before dark."

"Worst comes to worst we have our blankets." Rulan doesn't seem to be in a hurry. Now that they are at lower altitudes she's feeling much better. She is at home in the wilderness—she has always been roaming the wildernesses, always searching and always believing she will find something but always ending up empty-handed. That is her life.

He is astounded by her boldness and her serenity. "Aren't you afraid?"

"I have you to protect me, so why should I be

afraid?" she replies without hesitation. There is a gleam of womanly trust and a child's frankness in her dark, wide eyes.

Touched by those words, he says: "I really like to...sit down and talk!"

In the deepening afterglow of the sunset, prayer flags flutter in the wind in the distance—since time immemorial nomadic tribes have used them to call back the souls of their departed kin.

"I once thought of suicide," he blurts out, as he slackens his pace.

She snorts, unimpressed. "I was wondering what you wanted to talk about. It turns out you had in mind this trick that works only on naïve little girls!"

He laughs in reply. "I didn't know you were so bad!"

"Am I bad?" she asks, shaking her head nonchalantly. "I've always believed suicide to be a very normal thing. It's nothing to make a fuss about. Everyone has the right to choose the timing and the manner of his own departure from this world, just as one can choose clothes to wear and food to eat. Of course it would be perfect if we also had a choice in the matter of our birth."

She extends her arm straight out from her, holding the snow lotus she has picked, as if she had in her palm an exquisite idea. Squinting her eyes and slightly cocking her head she admires the soft yellow petals, all the more gorgeous and splendid in the last gleam of the sunset.

"Beautiful! Oh so beautiful!" Then she mutters: "No wonder the Buddhist bodhisattvas all sit on a lotus seat. It does make people think of the nirvana of the soul. All would-be suicides must first attain this transcendent state, or else they would not renounce..."

"Don't say a word more!" he stops her peremptorily, yanking her arm back. She stumbles and falls into his arms, whereupon he bends down and gives her a kiss behind her ear.

The kiss sends a tremor through her body and she feels as if she has been dropped into molten lava. She is full of confusion in her heart, of uncertainty in her mind, unclear about the meaning of the kiss and about what will happen next. Without quite realizing it, she raises her right hand, whether out of shyness or in a sign of rejection, and puts up a meaningless and lame resistance. Then his mouth finds her lips.

When he puts her down on the blanket, she says

in a soft, querulous tone: "You never said anything to me."

His only answer is a deep sigh that comes from the depth of his chest. Then he takes her to a previously unexplored territory in the ardent evening afterglow.

When they sit up again, they momentarily freeze at the sight of blood stains on the blanket. They blurt out simultaneously: "Sorry!"

Then Rulan looks away, and tears start streaming down her cheeks. Songlin is embarrassed and apologetic, at a loss about what to do. "Sorry, I didn't know."

She bites her lip and then says: "No, no, you will despise me. You must have nothing but scorn for me now!"

He spins her around and cups her chin in his hand. "Do I? Why should I despise you?"

"I..." Continuing through a haze of tears she says: "I was a reject, and nobody wanted me..."

He appears puzzled. Her disheveled hair cascades down her white neck to fall on her half bared, full breasts, which peek through with a pearly gleam. Looking at her, listening to her breathing and seeing her forlorn, helpless air, he feels the sense of being swept off his feet by a gale wind.

"Do you...do you still want me?" Like the rustling of the evening wind through the trees, a faint sigh escapes her quivering lips, softly, very softly.

He pauses for a moment before answering. In a flash he has understood everything and gives a clear, crisp reply as if in anger: "Yes, I do!"

9

The sun has sunk among the snow peaks of the Min mountain range and dusk is settling in. Chen Songlin leads Rulan along a trail bordered by rows of *Rhododendron watsonii*. At the end of the trail they are surprised to see a small, low mud hut.

Once inside the hut, Rulan lets out a startled cry: "It looks like someone has been here recently!"

Indeed, a thick layer of straw covers the floor. There is an extinguished stove. The mud walls are studded with wooden pegs on which hang yak horns, yak tails and medicinal herbs they do not recognize.

Dusk is falling fast. Looking out through the

small openings in the walls on the two sides of the hut, they can see the far peaks turning a purplish black. Faint snatches of a wistful tune played on a flute waft down from some ethnic Qiang settlement in the distance. For Rulan, seated on the straw matting, the mud hut feels like a time capsule, taking her back to somewhere primitive and heart-warming.

While Rulan is absorbed in her reverie, Songlin has already lit up a pile of dried cow dung near the stove.

"You seem surprisingly at home here." Then she can't resist the question: "Have you been here before?"

Casting a glance at the yak horns and the herbs on the walls, Songlin says evasively: "Do you mind if I smoke? In deference to you, I've refrained all these hours."

It is a rhetorical question, and she silently watches him in the light of the fire. He has an attractive profile—the strong, masculine lines, as if chiseled, of his nose and chin contrast with a mouth that exhibits a feminine softness.

"This is our home." He lights a Marlboro on the cow dung fire. "The first human home—a man and a woman keeping warm by a fire."

Touched by these words, she quietly moves closer, wreathing herself in the smoke he exhales. She suddenly realizes that the smoke is also light blue, her favorite color, and it has a pleasant smell. She is eager to inhale it. As she breathes it in, she feels a mysterious anticipation.

A silent expectancy is also discernible on his face. But what is he expecting? At the back of the hut is a slope overgrown with sandthorn scrub and under these bushes, snow lotuses are in blossom. Nature, in a state that has existed for ages, also appears to be breathing, expecting and listening for something in the crystal clear night.

"Ah—Long—"

There it goes again! The voice pierces the quiet of the night as if someone is crying out in his sleep. But it is not as eerie as on the previous occasions; now it sounds like musical notes played on a Qiang flute suddenly woven into a particularly sad melody.

Instinctively Rulan draws closer to Songlin. Putting a hand on his shoulder, she seems to want to say something or need something from him; but he remains sitting upright with a straight back, his cigarette pinched between his fingers. With this erect posture, his raised elbow and the glow of his cigarette, he is in a way saying no to her. "This voice is so familiar. It reminds me of someone…"

"Huang Gu Long?" Rulan's first impulse is to laugh, but the laugh will not come because she's seized by an emotion she cannot understand. "Do you know him?"

"No," Songlin shakes his head, "I am talking about a Wang Qiangba."

"What a strange name!" A slight frown appears on Rulan's brow. "Is he Tibetan Chinese?"

"No, he is Han Chinese. A Han with a Tibetan given name, Qiangba, but a Han surname. He roams the Huanglong Ravine and Songfan areas, making a living by collecting medicinal herbs. Nobody knows where he came from, but we detected in his Mandarin a southern accent—more specifically an accent of Jiangsu province…"

"Wait a minute," Rulan, like a little girl listening spellbound to a story, interrupts him. "What period are you talking about? How did you meet?"

"Oh, it was a long, long time ago." Giving his head a pat, Chen Songlin has a look of suddenly being transported back to a distant time. "I was in college then. I was sent down here to join the socialist education campaign. We had a girl in our class..."

"Was she a girlfriend?" Rulan asks with a smile.

Songlin continues, unsmiling and offering no denial: "She was from a bourgeois family and had a sheltered childhood. She was a city person so she knew nothing about rural life and everything was novel to her. When she saw a rooster mounting a hen, she thought they were fighting and tried to separate them. Some mischievous guys in the class would shout teasingly whenever the occasion arose: 'Jing Jing! The rooster is bullying the hen again. Go chase him off!'

"One holiday a group of us went to the Huanglong Temple on an outing. Jing Jing struck off alone toward the Huanglong Cave in front of the temple. In her excitement she failed to notice the cave entry right under her feet and she lost her footing. Luckily someone caught her in time— an herb collector dressed in black seemed to have sprung out of the ground and caught her in the nick of time.

"When Jing Jing saw the tracks made by her own feet on the ground, she was paralyzed with terror and for some time couldn't move. When her classmates hurried to her side, their faces blanched with fright. What they saw below them was a bottomless abyss. It gave them vertigo simply to glance into it.

"Then we remembered that for days the herb collector had followed us, by chance or intentionally. Now that he saved Jing Jing's life, we naturally wanted to know his name and he told us he was called Wang Qiangba."

"Maybe he made it up," Rulan blurts out.

Taking no notice of this last remark, Songlin continues, with a nod: "By winter recess when we were ready to head back to our respective cities, Wang Qiangba came to Jing Jing to tell her, falteringly, that he had a daughter with whom he had lost contact for more than ten years. He produced a slip of paper with an address on it, which was in Jing Jing's native city. She immediately knew where it was and promised she would help him find his daughter. Then Wang Qiangba remembered something and quickly wrote down another address and handed it to Jing Jing. He said their house might not be there anymore and his daughter might have followed her grandmother to their home in the countryside."

"Was she found?" Rulan asks anxiously, by now totally fascinated by the story.

Songlin shakes his head. "I lived in another city, so I had no idea what happened with her search. Anyway after we came back here at the end of winter recess, Jing Jing appeared to assiduously avoid Wang Qiangba. And Wang Qiangba showed up around here with greater frequency, watching Jing Jing with expectant eyes, wanting but fearing to ask the question on his mind.

"The situation became intolerable to me, so I said to Jing Jing, 'Even if you didn't find the daughter, at least you should tell him so that he will no longer be hounded by doubt.' Jing Jing let out a sigh—the first time I heard her sigh in such a manner. She said she did find her but it made her feel worse than if she had failed in her mission. His daughter had no wish at all to acknowledge him as her father. She said she didn't have a father like him. How could she tell him that? Jing Jing felt it was better to keep his hope alive..."

"Songlin!" Rulan throws herself on him and takes his cigarette away. But he lights another one. "Shortly afterwards, we received a secret arrest warrant from high up the chain of command. It was known to party members and student cadres only. The object of the arrest warrant was none other than Wang Qiangba, allegedly a rightist who had slipped through the dragnet of the anti-rightist campaign and was a counterrevolutionary on the run. I lost no time in quietly alerting Jing Jing, telling her to sift through all her belongings to see if they contained anything linking her to Wang Qiangba, such as addresses in his handwriting, and to burn them all so that she wouldn't be implicated. But Jing Jing went that night to warn Wang Qiangba and he went on the run again.

"Wang Qiangba disappeared without a trace into the mountains but Jing Jing was charged. A mass meeting was called to denounce her. Everyone was required to speak at the meeting and state his position on the matter. I couldn't wriggle out of the obligation, all the more so because I was the one who leaked the information to her. If my attitude was considered unacceptable, I would be criticized and charged with a crime.

"So I had no choice but to go on stage to denounce and criticize her. After the criticism meeting, she mysteriously disappeared. My other classmates and I went out looking for her the whole night. When day broke, someone found a wet handkerchief in front of the Huanglong Cave and signs of disturbance at its entrance. It was concluded that she had jumped into the pit to her death."

While the coldness of his tone indicates that he is telling a story of an ancient past, dead and buried, a glistening wetness begins to form at the corners of his eyes. Rulan reaches out to wipe it away and says in a whisper: "I understand."

"What do you understand?"

She leaves the question unanswered. Through the blue curling smoke she sees a thin, sallow little girl. In the wintry cold of January she's wearing an old cotton quilted jacket whose sleeves cover her arms only to the elbow. She is making a great effort to hold the pencil with her little hand, red and swollen with the freezing cold, as she hunches over her homework on the classroom desk. This crude room, with walls that cannot keep out cold drafts, is what serves as a rural elementary school. At recess all the kids have rushed off except her. She remains in her seat, racking her brain to find a solution to an arithmetic problem.

All of a sudden her classmates throng about her. "Lan Lan, there is a pretty auntie looking for you.

We told her you were here and she gave us candies. She still has a bunch of candies, with cellophane wrappers!"

She raises her head and immediately experiences a shock: this is the first time she has seen a full-length black wool coat and a rose-red wool scarf of such elegance! The face, smooth and white like porcelain, is smiling affectionately at her. "Are you Huang Rulan? Your father..."

The moment she hears the mention of "father," the little girl jumps up as if stung by a scorpion. "I don't have a father, go away!"

Instead of walking away, the pretty auntie comes up to her and puts a hand on her arm. "Everyone has a father. How can you not have one? Your father lives in a faraway place and he misses you very much but he cannot come back to visit you. Can you write a few words to him?"

The lady's voice is soft and pleasant. She puts a fountain pen in the little girl's hand. It is so beautiful with its shiny violet barrel.

With the fountain pen in her hand the little girl presses her lips together, almost persuaded. Suddenly she grits her teeth and throws the pen on the floor before turning around and running off.

She runs all the way home. Pushing the door open she sees her grandmother sitting on a small stool, wiping away tears with a corner of her garment. She asks with incomprehension: "Grandma, are you crying?"

"No, no, some dust got into my eyes." Grandma quickly rises to her feet. "Lan Lan, you must be hungry. Grandma will cook you some taro porridge."

She shakes her head, then seeing a bag of cellophane-wrapped candies on the table, she asks suspiciously: "Did a pretty auntie come?"

"Oh, did she go to your school?" Grandma asks anxiously. "What did you say to her? What did you say?"

Seeing her grandmother's anxiety, she hastens to reassure her: "Grandma, I have not forgotten your instruction. I didn't say anything. I told her I didn't have a father." It's only then that her grandmother breathes a sigh of relief. "Good child, remember, in the future no matter who asks you, you must always give the same answer. If you gave the wrong answer in a slip of the tongue, you would forfeit any chance of getting admitted to high school. If you couldn't get into high school, your father..."

Realizing her mistake, Grandma gives herself a slap on the face, saying: "Oh Grandma was wrong! Grandma was wrong! Lan Lan, you must always say: I have no father, no father, no father..."

As she says this, Grandma's wizened lips tremble. Seeing this, little Lan Lan is scared. As Grandma's lips tremble they start to droop to one side and the color drains out of them.

"Grandma, don't you worry! I will remember it, always!" She is so frightened she can no longer suppress her shriek.

But Grandma appears possessed as white froth bubbles out of the corners of her mouth, and her lips, slate-colored by now, keep trembling. "You don't have a father, you don't..." Then she lists to one side and collapses on the floor.

Rulan will never forget these last words of her kind and gentle grandmother before she left both her and the world: "You don't have a father, you don't!"

"I don't have a father, I don't!" Repeating these words in her mind, she gives her head a shake, as if determined to brush away all illusions and all the ideas that keep crowding in on her.

10

"Tell me! What did you understand? Huh? What did you understand?" Chen Songlin persists.

"I have come to understand Jing Jing and I've come to understand you." Rulan takes a long breath. "I've come to understand the black hole in your life."

"Rulan!"

"Grandma called me Lan Lan."

"Lan Lan..."

"Shhh, be quiet," she says placing her index finger against her lips. "Jing Jing lives on in your heart. I can see her there."

"What does she look like?" Songlin is sure she can't answer the question.

"An alabaster complexion, a noble forehead and a beautiful, straight nose, large, dark attractive eyes. She looked at you with a sincerity and affection, a warmth and kindness that were already rare in those times." Rulan's eyes are half closed as if in a kind of trance.

Songlin is dumbfounded. "How...how did you

know?"

Ignoring him, Rulan continues: "She was refined and charming. She liked to wear a black wool coat matched with a rose-red scarf—colors that remind one of night as dense as soil and the earliest flower to break out of that deep, dark soil, like the sun of early dawn. It's something that greets your eyes every day and that's why you are constantly reminded of her. You will never forget her."

"You!" Chen Songlin's jaw drops, and he cries, forgetting himself: "Who are you? Have you met her?"

Shaking her head, Rulan reopens her eyes and looks at him with a glimmer in her eyes. "I have special powers. I can see traces she's left behind in you."

His eyes hold hers for a moment, then he suddenly drops his cigarette and takes her into his arms. It is a tight, savage embrace. Kisses rain on her like a summer downpour. "Dearest, I love you, I love you, I love you..."

This truly feels like love! In comparison the specks of blood on the blanket meant nothing.

But she still lacks confidence. "Really? Why?"

Ignoring the question, he starts unbuttoning her

blouse with fingers that shake. "Have you heard about Tantric Buddhism?"

She shakes her head.

Then he asks: "Do you know why Sakyamuni, the Buddha, sits on a lotus?"

She shakes her head again. She feels her strength and her voice have deserted her.

"Tantric Buddhists advocate the union of man and woman as a means to enlightenment. They believe the creation and propagation of all beings in the world depends on the sexual prowess of the gods."

When the last impediment has been removed, the woman's body is revealed, at 42 years of age still showing jade-like purity, freshness and smoothness. Its snow white immaculateness and perfect sinuosity would be ideal for life drawing class. He mutters to himself in disbelief: "My goddess—something's not right!"

"Huh?" she moans softly. "What's not right?"

"Your age—I mean, your actual age versus the age you appear to be. No, no, I mean the age shown on the surface of your body and..." He is becoming incoherent and his breathing quickens.

"I exercise everyday," she says, blushing like a

little girl. "I strive for perfection."

"Ah, I understand!" He gives a chuckle like a naughty boy. "All this time you've been making yourself perfect for me."

Suddenly he falls silent.

Just then the saintly clarion call of a bell in some Buddhist lamasery ripples across the night sky. They float and drift, lost in a vast field of snow lotuses, experiencing sensations of cold and heat; cold as pure petals opening in the snow and hot as the ardent sun at its zenith.

As they alternate between cold and hot, they also feel like crying and laughing.

"The lotus, the cradle in which the female sex procreates life," Songlin says, panting. "Sakyamuni... is born out of a lotus."

The vitality of life erupts, radiating heat, which, like sunlight penetrating the snow lotus, sets aquiver the pistil buried deep down in the flower. Rulan sobs softly: "I remember now, today is my birthday. I think...I think I have a father after all."

Day 4

In the Midst of
the Gold Rush

1

An early riser by habit, Xu Youzhi, accompanied by
Xing Xing, has left Jiuzhaigou by car at first light. It is
only ten in the morning when they arrive in Songfan.

Not one to sit around waiting for things to
happen, the moment they settled in at the hotel he
sent Xing Xing to find out about Sha Sha and the
others. As she had been instructed by Songlin, Xing
Xing went to the county government seat to check
the latest news but came away empty-handed.

"Oh, Sha Sha has ruined this writers'
meeting. What an annoyance!" In front of Xing
Xing, Xu Youzhi doesn't feel the need to hide his

disgruntlement.

"There's so much fun to be had in Jiuzhaigou!" Pouting her little mouth, shaped like a water chestnut, Xing Xing makes no secret of her annoyance either. "We only got to stay there one day and there's no knowing when we'll get to come back for another visit!"

"Next time I will absolutely refuse to bring a secretary like her!" Xu Youzhi says in ill humor.

Xing Xing chuckles. "Mr. Xu, you sound like you are coming back for another visit."

"So what if I do!" Xu Youzhi retorts. "If I want to come back, I'll come. It's as simple as that."

Upon reflection, Xing Xing agrees: the government has relaxed restrictions on travel between the mainland and Taiwan, and he has plenty of money. So if the fancy takes him he can just hop on a plane and come. It's very simple indeed for him. "But," she says to herself, "we mainlanders who are born here and die here are rooted to our designated corner like a tree, with little chance to budge from it."

However it's the tree's roots that retain the nutrients and water. That is an unalterable fact. Xing

Xing suddenly gives a cheerful cry like a child: "Do bring us back here for another visit!"

"Sure," Xu Youzhi drawls heartily, "I promise to bring you with me. But I am tired now. I need a nap. You go and have some rest too."

"No, I don't want to." Xing Xing shakes her head. "I'll stay here and read and take care of you. What if you get sick again?"

"Nonsense! Why would I be sick again?" He feigns anger but pulls her to him and kisses her on the forehead. "Good girl—that's enough, now go!"

"Didn't you say you never kissed girls?" Xing Xing asks mischievously.

"You talk too much!"

"Why don't you want to kiss girls? There has to be a reason." Xing Xing refuses to let it go. "Ah, yes, last night you said you were carrying Meng Long in your arms and you were going to kill yourself. What happened after that?"

"After that?" He blinks his eyes, puts a hand on his bald head and says with a blank expression: "Did I die? Hmm, did I die after that?"

"You are naughty, naughty, Mr. Xu!" Xing Xing is very much frustrated at being kept in suspense but

Xu Youzhi closes his eyes in exhaustion.

But he no longer feels sleepy now as he remembers with clarity the frightened and panicky cries that Meng Long uttered as he stormed out of the Huanglong Temple carrying her in his arms.

"Stop!"

Yes, that was her cry. And at that exact moment he looked down and realized that they were only a few feet away from a precipice.

The valley floor below was shrouded in a mist of the same soft whiteness as the pale sky; the abyss and the sky beckoned with equal intensity. He ordered: "Be still!" Dignified and dour, he continued to walk, not looking back for a moment. "This is home— home for you and me!"

She stopped struggling, instead locking him in a tight hug and kissing the grim-mouthed young man on his lips.

As if jolted by an electric shock, he felt his legs turn to water and he could not take another step. Instinctively he held her tighter but his heart continued to resist and he still refused to open his lips.

When her soft tender tongue thrust against his

teeth, he was seized by such a heady, sweet sensation that he gave up all resistance. No sooner did his mouth open a crack than her tongue darted deftly in, igniting a fire whose blazing flames melted ice and thawed snow. His skin, muscles, bones, the blood coursing through his body, his neural network—all were dissolved. He no longer knew anything, no longer could do anything. He collapsed holding her in his arms at the brink of the cliff, moaning and muttering: "Let's die together! Let's die!"

When he picked himself up at the edge of the cliff, he felt he had taken her within him. He had filled his own heart with her life. His new life had just begun.

The sun rose, its millions of rays penetrating the sky and the snow peaks, fusing the blue and the white into a single boundless new life. The bright red flowers of the rhododendron were in full bloom everywhere, underneath trees, in the cracks between rocks on the travertine hillsides and in the cold highland. When these flowers bloom, they burst forth with all their youthful energy going into the flowers, unaccompanied by green leaves. They spread like a blazing fire of hope, splashing the ascending dragon with a palette of brilliant colors, giving it life.

Hand in hand, they explored the hills. They talked, embraced and kissed in the forest, on the yellow dragon's claws, and by turquoise cascading pools. The bright sunshine of the highland enriched both passion and color; emotions and hopes flamed with heightened purity.

At nightfall they found lodging in a Qiang settlement. In return for a small sum the hospitable Qiang folk served them a local specialty of chicken braised with a certain type of thin noodle, and later put them up in a small mud hut in the forest. It had once served as a dormitory for forest guards.

Neither mentioned Gu Long, or the Huanglong Temple, or even the trip to Yan'an. As past and future fell away, only the sweet joys of the moment sparkled like champagne bubbles.

"Mr. Xu, why have you fallen silent?" Xing Xing tugs at his elbow like a child. "What happened after that?"

After that?

He presses his temples with his hands. After that—after that, when he had his young bride in his arms on their nuptial night, and whenever he made love to women he met in chance encounters during his numerous trips, he would close his eyes and pretend they were Meng Long; and the most luxurious bedroom would morph into that mud hut in the forest. He still remembers the slope behind the hut, covered with sandthorn shrubs, their green leaves pointing straight up as if every one of their veins was rising in revolt, as if they wanted to lift into space. Underneath the sandthorns grew a scattering of snow lotuses. The snow on the sandthorns had not yet thawed completely and cold beads of melted snow dripped from their sword-like twigs onto the lotuses that broke through the frozen ground. Nourished by the cold drops (they felt warm to those new growths used to frigid soil), the tender yellow petals soon opened up. Like golden flutes the pistils played, up there on high, a tremulous, impassioned tune that broke through the barriers of the cold and brought tears and smiles to the people's faces. Due to this quality, the snow lotus has widely been associated with pure love in the popular imagination.

"After that—we had a baby." Turning his head around he gazes at Xing Xing, surprised by the simplicity of it all.

"Wow! Great!" Xing Xing cheers. "So you got married?"

"No, we did not." Xu Youzhi shakes his head. "I was a dissolute bounder. Not only did I not marry her, I didn't even know she was pregnant. We soon went our separate ways."

"Why?" Xing Xing asks with wide-eyed curiosity.

"There didn't seem to be any particular reason." Xu Youzhi pauses, patting his head. "She was obsessed with the idea of going to Yan'an but I already lost that urge."

"Oh, I understand." Xing Xing nods gravely. "You were no longer fellow travelers on the revolutionary path, so you parted ways."

"Rubbish!" But instead of taking offense, Xu Youzhi chuckles. "There's one more thing. That day Gu Long set out to look for Meng Long and hurt his leg in a fall. Lying in a gully he kept calling out for me. The call echoed through the mountains and valleys: Ah Long—Ah Long..."

"So that's why every time you heard the cry for Ah Long, you thought it was Gu Long and you became ill?" Xing Xing blurts out.

Xu Youzhi grunts distractedly. Xing Xing

quickly adds: "It can't possibly be him. It must be your imagination."

"Of course—after all it has been forty years," Xu Youzhi says with a deep frown. "But this voice was too familiar. It had to be Gu Long. No one else would cry like that."

"Oh, you left because Gu Long found Meng Long again?" Xing Xing is a shrewd girl. After giving some thought to the matter, she goes on to ask, "So where did you go after that?"

Fate works in mysterious ways! For all these years he has kept even his wife in the dark about this but now he is spilling his secrets to this young girl. "After leaving the two of them, I asked myself where I could go from there. Then an idea hit me. I figured, since the government was trying to track us down, and since the least likely place to attract the attention of the people on our heels was the government's own ranks, that would be the safest place for me. So I decided to join the army."

"You mean the KMT government's army?"

"Of course!"

Xing Xing stares fixedly at Xu Youzhi, at his shiny bald crown, the wrinkled forehead, and tries to imagine the dashing, naughty, passionate and devoted young man of yesteryear. Then a look of having been startled out of a dream comes into her eyes, which begin to moisten. "You are so smart, Mr. Xu! If I had lived in that era, I would have fallen in love with you—your smart head!"

A chuckle escapes the lips of Xu Youzhi and he says, pointing at his head: "I've not been beheaded. So this is the same head. Do you love it?"

Xing Xing blushes and stamps her feet coquettishly: "You are twisting my words!"

"Huh?" Xu Youzhi blinks his eyes, rolling his head right and left on the pillow, and says with a straight face: "Did I say something wrong?"

Xing Xing laughs with him and playfully touches his bald head with her delicate hand. Xu Youzhi pulls her into his arms.

2

Xing Xing leans her cheek against his chest and feels as if she were six years old again—when her father held her in his arms in the shade of a tree to escape the heat. Frightened by a caterpillar crawling on a leaf, she clung tighter to him. Her father said, patting her skinny shoulder: "There's nothing to be afraid of, nothing to be afraid of!" And fear left her. She felt warm and safe as she cuddled up against his broad, strong chest.

As time went on her father's face became emaciated and his muscular chest shriveled. He looked skeletal and his eyes became shifty. And he was only in his fifties.

When she had to speak to her father about something, she always averted her face because she was repulsed by the ever-present stench of chicken feathers about him, his gummed up eyes and the hairs protruding from his nostrils. She couldn't imagine she had once nestled against his chest.

One day her father, who had had too much to drink, staggered into the kitchen to get a drink of water. The so-called kitchen was really only a lean-to built with sheets of tar paper against the back of the house. She was bathing herself in the kitchen with a stool propped against the door. When her father pushed the door, the stool crashed to the floor, and her father, in a tipsy stupor, picked up his daughter from the tub and took the dripping girl to his bed...

She was seventeen.

In time she gave herself to Songlin. The not-so-sturdy chest of Songlin was like a sampan in motion, giving her dizziness, pleasure and hope. But she has known with certainty that he is not her destiny, but a sampan only, a sampan that will ferry her from one shore to another.

Now she finds the embrace of this Mr. Xu from Taiwan calm as a haven and toasty as a hot water bottle. Nestled against him, she experiences an unprecedented sense of fulfillment and satisfaction. That thumping heart seems to say to her: "Don't be afraid! No caterpillar dares to bite you now."

She suddenly starts sobbing as she remembers those chicken feathers, the bathing incident, the humble dorm room with its hard plank bed, and all those nights of hard study. She clings tightly to him, calling him "Daddy."

"Good girl, good girl!" He strokes her gently. She is now able to see more clearly the deep lines that seam his face and the emerging age spots—he is not her father, and he is older than her father, but what does it matter? The warm embrace of someone older gives her a sense that she is once again a delicate and helpless baby, and helps her forget all the strife and chaos in the troublesome world out there. It makes her realize that this is what she has long craved—a lighthouse, a man that stands tall.

Her mind is a little confused at this moment and she has yet to compose her thoughts. It is true that she has taken great pains to ingratiate herself with him and that she is obsessed with the idea of traveling abroad. But at this moment these thoughts have given way to the feeling that all her past efforts have been a preparation for this soothing balm.

"Are you a virgin?" he asks her.

She nods, sobbing.

"Don't worry," he hugs her tighter, "Daddy will not ruin that."

"No, no," she suddenly starts to cry in earnest. She grinds her little head into his chest and her tears leave wet stains on his shirt: "No no, Daddy, I love you, Daddy, I want you..."

"My baby, listen, listen to me." Xu Youzhi strokes her face and wipes off the tears. "Daddy also likes you and wants you, but Daddy can't...Get up! Sit here and talk to Daddy."

She sits up reluctantly, hurt written across her face. She starts to say something but checks herself. Her sobs die down gradually. He says to her: "Yesterday Daddy's sudden illness must have given you a fright. Daddy will make it up to you by giving you a belated birthday party."

"A birthday party?" With residual tears still in her eyes, she says, "My birthday is long past."

"Silly girl!" he says, kissing her. "Now that you are my daughter, you will have my daughter's birthday."

"Your daughter's birthday was yesterday?" Xing Xing is still confused.

"You bet!" Xu Youzhi says with some satisfaction. "A propitious day, because it coincides with the birthday of Sakyamuni."

Xing Xing is thinking back to the details of his story. "Hey, didn't you join the army? The KMT government's army?"

"Yes," Xu Youzhi heaves a sigh. "I went to Taiwan after joining the army. I had to wait forty years for this homecoming."

"Then how did you find out your daughter's birthday?" Xing Xing's curiosity is piqued anew.

"My Meng Long, she wrote me about it," says Xu

Youzhi softly. "In the early 1950s, I received a letter from her through an intermediary in Hong Kong. In the letter Meng Long told me she became a war correspondent after she arrived in Yan'an and Gu Long got involved in propaganda. They got married shortly after. When the communists gained control of the whole country, they returned to civilian life. The party got her a job with a magazine publisher and made Gu Long the principal of a high school."

"And after that?" asks Xing Xing, with impatient curiosity.

"After that they both got into some trouble." His answer is a little vague.

"No, I was asking about your daughter," she reminds him.

"Oh, my daughter!" Getting up he nudges her aside as he makes his way to the window and parts the curtain, letting in a flood of sunshine. The light stings his eyes. He will never forget the day he read Meng Long's letter. He was on a noisy beach. Fishermen's kids ran around, giving cheerful cries whenever silvery catches were hauled in. Meng Long told him that she and Gu Long were never close again after he found out she had a child by someone else. The setting sun low on the horizon on the other side of the Strait sent up a blood-red afterglow and he, like a helpless orphan, gazed out toward the far shore, and his eyes grew dim with burning tears.

3

When Songlin and Rulan arrive, Mr. Xu is talking to Xing Xing about helping to get her into a school in the United States. Xing Xing seems to be in a dreamy state. She had never imagined that Xu Youzhi would take a personal interest in her studies. He told her he liked young people who study hard and is in favor of students traveling outside their own country to broaden their horizons. He said that his daughter in Taiwan would go to the United States after graduating college.

As he continues, the spell is suddenly broken by Chen Songlin's anxious tone: "Sha Sha hasn't been found, so Rulan and I had to go to the public security bureau of Songfan county for help."

"What did they say at the bureau?" Xu Youzhi turns to Songlin, his eyebrows raised sharply.

"When they learned that the missing person was a young lady from Taiwan, they got very concerned," Chen Songlin replies. "These days they happen to be organizing a crackdown on bands of separatists. The search and arrest operation covers a large area, so the police have given the task force the extra task of helping to find Sha Sha. They don't think it will be a problem because they are conducting a robust, meticulous operation. Unless she had some kind of accident, Sha Sha will be found."

"Oh we have been more of a hindrance than a help!" Xu Youzhi paces the floor in dejection, his hands clasped behind him.

Rulan casts a glance his way and starts to say something, but decides instead to make a suggestion to Chen Songlin: "If we wait here, we'll only get frustrated. Let's go out there and look around. Perhaps..."

She has barely begun her sentence, when Xu Youzhi expresses his agreement: "She's right. Let's get out there."

The small mountain village appears to have only one narrow street, which leads to a bridge and a dam. Xu Youzhi sets off in great strides. No one knows where he's heading, so they move to stay close behind him.

Unlike this group, which travels at a hurried pace, ahead of them on a stone bridge, approaching in a leisurely fashion, is a figure wrapped in free-flowing garb, a pair of large, curved, black horns on her head!

Xing Xing, who has sharp eyes, is the first to recognize the figure. "Hey! Isn't that Sha Sha?"

Sha Sha recognizes them at the same moment and jubilantly holds up the yak horns: "Look! Guys, look!"

Her friends, hugely relieved, do not have the heart to scold her, except Xu Youzhi. His face hardens, and he is ready to fly into a rage, but Sha Sha has already thrust the horns right under his nose. "Take a look! These are real yak horns. You can lug them home and I'm sure your two sons will love them."

Taking the horns from her, Xu Youzhi passes his hand over them, forgetting he was going to give her a tongue-lashing, and narrows his eyes in a burgeoning smile. "Where did you get them?"

Sha Sha triumphantly looks from one to the other before she announces, stressing each word: "Uncle Gu Long gave them to me!"

"What? What did you say?" Everyone is taken aback, but it's Xu Youzhi who undergoes the most dramatic change of expression.

Ignoring the question, Sha Sha turns toward Chen Songlin and gives a cheer, throwing her arms in the air. "It's so great, your theory of creative writing! It has enabled me to conceive a novel! I'm serious! I have the material for a novel!"

"I don't care about novels or short stories," Xu Youzhi says impatiently. "Tell me! Who did you run into?"

"Mr. Xu, have some patience!" Sha Sha makes a face, giggling. "I have found your Gu Long for you, so you owe me a big thank you!"

She fishes out of her pocket a sheet of paper and shows it to Chen Songlin. It is covered with densely spaced writing. "This is the outline of the novel I've conceived following the guidelines of your theory of creative writing. Wow! Uncle Gu Long's life story is incredibly outlandish, so full of plot twists and crammed with information. I had to add extra axes. Look! This X-axis indicates..."

"Enough! That's enough!" Xu Youzhi waves his hand impatiently. "Quit talking about creative writing. Tell me first how you ran into Gu Long. What did he say to you?"

"Last night I got lost and fell into a gully. I passed out—" Sha Sha starts now to recount her adventure in detail. "An herb collector rescued me. He carried me up to the highway and waved down a tour bus, which took me to the hospital in Songfan. The hospital found nothing seriously wrong with me, so the old man brought me to his home."

"What does he look like? How old is he?" Xu Youzhi presses her, anxious to find out.

"The old man wears black clothes from head to toe, and only his hair and beard are white. He looks like a savage but from up close he seems to possess the aura of a fairy god.

"He asked me where I was from, why I walked in these uninhabited mountains by myself. I told him I was from Taiwan and I was here on a tour, and because I kept hearing someone calling for my Ah Loong, I had left my group and followed the voice there. Unexpectedly he sighed and told me he had also been looking for his Ah Long for three days now and figured he'd never find him. I asked him who this Ah Long of his was to him.

"He said Ah Long was a homeless kid he'd found and they had lived together for many years. During the day he would gather herbs and Ah Long would herd sheep. In the evening he taught the boy to read. He had saved up some money to give the kid a chance for a better future, and was planning to send the boy out of these mountains this fall to receive an education..."

"Young lady, can you cut to the chase please?" Xu Youzhi begs Sha Sha out of frustration.

"All right, all right." Sha Sha decides to take another tack, skipping over many details: "Last night I stayed by a small stream in his humble hut, which he built himself at the edge of town using wood planks. The wind was blowing hard outside but he had cow dung burning and we kept warm by the fire like primitives, our distorted shadows dancing on the wall.

"None of you would believe that this old savage was once a college student and the principal of a high school. Now that his Ah Long had disappeared, he said he lost any interest in venturing out of the house. He said there was so much he needed to say before it was too late but time was running out. So he decided he might as well tell all of it to me, a stranger from Taiwan.

"When he spoke, he remained almost still. Even when he broke the dried cow dung into small chunks and fed them into the fire, his movement was slow and deliberate. The flames threw flickering patches of light and shadow across his sallow face and black clothes. His long, untidy white hair and beard seemed almost in danger of being singed by the fire. His appearance reminded me of a ceramic with its glaze showing fine cracks, fired into the hardness of iron and taking on an antique look from long disuse. Time seemed to have evaporated before him—really, for him time has no substance, having been reduced to a string of numbers: 49, 50, 54, 57, 58 years..."

"Did he arrive here in early 1958 when he fled from Shanghai?" Chen Songlin can no longer hold the question back.

"Yes, yes!" Sha Sha becomes excited. "He mentioned something about 1957, some anti-rightist...campaign. Hey Songlin, why did you have so many political campaigns in the mainland? And with every campaign people suffered. Even a savage living out here away from civilization could not escape the destruction. I added a separate axis for the 'political campaigns' he described to me. Take a look at this. Did I list them correctly?"

As Sha Sha reads off the campaigns on the list, Rulan clasps her arm. "Dear Sha Sha! Can you take us to that man?"

Turning her face toward Rulan, Sha Sha sees in her eyes an anxious expectancy, which is unusual given her customary aloofness, and feels the trembling in the hand that clutches her arm. She beams with satisfaction. "Our great writer! You have been deeply moved and you want to dig up some material, right? That will not do. You can't do that. I own a patent on it."

"Sha Sha!" Xu Youzhi gives an order that brooks no disobedience, "Take us to him! Now!"

4

"What's the hurry?" In the car, Sha Sha yawns and stretches out of fatigue. "He's been here for more than thirty years. Do you think he might run away from one day to the next?"

Xing Xing is inclined to agree with Sha Sha but the grimness on all the faces and the tension in the air discourage her from risking censure by siding with Sha Sha. She gives a quiet nudge to Mr. Xu with her elbow signaling a wish to say something but he appears not to take any notice. He continues to gaze out at the landscape rushing by, his eyebrows, thick and black despite his age, tightly furrowed, and his already narrow eyes squeezed into even narrower slits.

It finally dawns on her that at this moment she has no place in his heart. He is not really her father. But of all these people, she is the only one privy to his thoughts: he believes that by finding Gu Long he will find Meng Long, and when he finds Meng Long he will find out about his daughter. However given that Gu Long has lived here in seclusion for over thirty years, clearly it is a tenuous hope at best.

But Xu Youzhi hangs on to this hope and rushes, body and mind, headlong into it, like a moth flying straight into a candle's flame. She wonders at the strength of the bond of blood.

What about romantic love? Is romantic love so fragile, so ephemeral?

A deep sadness arises in her heart. She half closes

her eyes—thinking back to her own biological father, to her mother who begged Xing Xing on her knees to keep the scandal within the family, and to the countless times she spoke to people in a buoyant and bubbly manner when she was aching inside. Family bonds? She shakes her head; she doesn't believe in the concept. It is an ornament worn on the breast of the wealthy.

Xing Xing opens her eyes at Sha Sha's cry: "Hey, we are here." Gu Long lives not far from the county seat, a ten-minute drive from their hotel.

They have to walk the rest of the way because from this point the road is unsuitable for automobiles. Sha Sha becomes excited again: "Look! That is the log cabin of Uncle Gu Long. Come! This way!"

Xing Xing brings up the rear, feeling lonely. Sha Sha's excited voice fills the air: "Listening to Uncle Gu Long, you feel as if history is opening right in front of your eyes, unfolding like a long hand scroll painting— it's both a wonderful and a painful experience."

To Xing Xing's ear, this voluble young lady from Taiwan suffers from a common human hypocrisy and false sentimentality: life can only be enjoyable and truly savored if it is steeped in a juice of pain and suffering. If that juice is not on hand, then you blend it yourself. But Xing Xing knows that real suffering is not a liquid but a solid, a hard rock that weighs down mercilessly on you. The only way to survive is to use the last strength in you to lift it off.

Maybe, even as you struggle to lift off one rock after another, you continue to mix another one of those drinks and imbibe it the way you would liquor. That's the way life treats you!

The fact is, of all these people (although they themselves are unaware of it), only Xing Xing and Sha Sha are unrelated to that mysterious Uncle Gu Long, and only they can talk and listen with unhurried ease, and mix that glass of perfectly colored liquid with elegance.

Xing Xing would share Sha Sha's cheery mood and run about excitedly like her, if only Mr. Xu would continue to take a personal interest in her and call her his "daughter." She would share his worries and pray for him, and drink from that glass with tears in her eyes, gaining in the process the satisfaction of having bestowed love and compassion.

Maybe Xu Youzhi is not intentionally neglecting her. But it is precisely this heartfelt "unintentionality" that causes her despair. She finds herself alone, separated from the rest of the crowd. She strolls up to the little log cabin and surveys the few conifers surrounding it, a patch by the house planted with scraggly highland barley, and a lone banner tied to a bamboo pole near the door—is this a prayer flag? She finds it pathetic, there all alone. In all the ethnic Tibetan hamlets along the way the houses were fronted by a sea of prayer flags fluttering in the wind, a striking sight in the highland.

Those who entered the cabin first emerge from it: "Uncle Gu Long is not here."

"How come?" Sha Sha refuses to believe it and ransacks the interior of the house looking for clues, even lifting the lids of cooking pots as if she would find someone hiding inside.

Songlin has an eye for details. "Sha Sha! Why is the earthen platform bed stripped bare? Was this *kang* like this yesterday?"

"There was a blanket on the *kang* yesterday!" Sha Sha cries in alarm. "I remember there was also an animal skin blanket, which is very warm."

"That means he has pulled up stakes and left for good," Songlin says thoughtfully.

5

"Left for good? You mean he ran away? But he was here only yesterday!" Xu Youzhi, who has kept silent until then, suddenly turns on Chen Songlin and starts yelling at him, as if Songlin were the cause of Gu Long's flight.

"I'm sorry, Mr. Xu," Songlin mutters, "it was only a guess."

Dismissing the explanation, Xu Youzhi angrily paces the floor and growls and pounces like a caged beast. "Sha Sha said he'd been living here for thirty years—and for all those years it never occurred to him to run away. So why did he run away today? Why? Huh? Why? Tell me—tell me!"

Nobody speaks—everyone looks at him, quietly feeling his despair and deep pain.

It's only after a long interval that Chen Songlin speaks up, cautiously: "We cannot be absolutely certain that this Uncle Gu Long never left this place in all those thirty some years. It would not be so extraordinary if he had gone away today to attend to some business."

Like a police dog with special sniffing abilities, Xu Youzhi observes Chen Songlin for the best part of a minute as he delivers his faltering words. Then he cuts him off abruptly: "You seem to know something—tell me, where has he gone?"

Chen Songlin shakes his head with a rueful smile. "Mr. Xu, like you, I am worried and I am anxious to find him."

"Maybe he went up the mountain to gather herbs. Let's set out again to look for him," Sha Sha suggests helpfully, despite her fatigue.

"You don't know anything about this place, so you shut up!" Xu Youzhi does not deign to even glance at Sha Sha but continues to fix his gaze on Chen Songlin, saying: "No, you are not like me. You must know something I don't."

Songlin sighs in resignation. "I told you it was only my guess. I think he can't possibly have gone far. He will probably have gone in the direction of Huanglong Ravine..."

"Oh, why are you so fond of hedging your bets?" Xu Youzhi cuts him off unceremoniously. "I don't want to hear 'possibly' or 'probably.' I need certainty—I must find him!"

To this unreasonable, dictatorial demand Chen Songlin replies: "All right, we'll do our best."

At Chen Songlin's suggestion the group returns to the hotel, packs and immediately sets out from Songfan. It falls to him to tell the driver where to go. Nobody asks where he's taking them, not even the stubborn, ill-tempered Xu Youzhi.

Like an old horse that knows its way, the tour bus takes Xu Youzhi into a vaguely familiar world. He sees a setting sun, its rays penetrating the blue sky and the snow peaks. How he misses his daughter! Even though on the other side of the Taiwan Strait he has been blessed with a happy family, he cannot stop thinking of the daughter he left behind on the mainland. In his imagination he has modeled her in the image of Xing Xing.

The bus stops at an elevation of 4,000 meters. They descend into a primeval wilderness carpeted by patches of green lichen and damp, black soil. Strewn about are chunks of a kind of half melted, half solid crystalline substance comprised equally of snow and ice, which gives off a white glint and is crunchy and soft underfoot. In spots reached by the sunlight are masses of little yellow dandelions, and foot-high snow lotuses peek out from under sandthorn bushes like so many golden candles lit up by the sun.

Stupefied, Rulan nearly cries out—isn't that the trail, bordered by bushes of rhododendrons, that leads down to the mud hut where she stayed with Chen Songlin last night?

6

The mud hut appears to be part of the soil—maybe this is why it is continually rebuilt even after it collapses. Through the vagaries of time, this primitive dwelling remains standing, a part of nature like the sandthorn bushes on the hardscrabble hill and the snow lotuses breaking out of the tundra.

The lack of oxygen in the highland causes a tightness in Xu Youzhi's chest, but despite his shortness of breath he moves at a brisk pace and is the first to reach the trail bordered by rhododendrons.

Rulan follows closely behind, still unable to get over her shock. Out of the blue Xu Youzhi points to a cluster of bright red rhododendrons in the sun: "My child, aren't these rhododendron flowers splendid!"

Rulan looks in perplexity over her shoulder but sees no one because the others haven't caught up with them. She realizes then that Xu Youzhi is addressing her. This executive from Taiwan has a habit of calling young people "my child" when he is excited.

"Yes, they are splendid! Splendid!" Rulan feels a little uneasy and somewhat touched. She even detects an unusual thump of her heart—no one has ever called her "my child" nor has anyone ever spoken to her in such an affectionate tone. She bends down to look at the flowers and seems to sense a call of flesh and blood in their bright red color. Could that mysterious Gu Long really be her father? It would be so incredible!

"Some say these flowers are a symbol." Xu Youzhi goes on enthusiastically: "What do they symbolize? What do you think they symbolize?"

"Yes, they are a symbol," Rulan answers haltingly. She seems to want to submit to his will, losing in the process her ability to think for herself and her usual pride. She doesn't know why it is so, but she willingly defers to his views. She continues vaguely: "Here in mainland China we used to have an opera called *Rhododendron Mountain* in which rhododendrons symbolize the heroism of revolutionaries."

When she realizes how inane that remark is, she falls silent and casts a glance at Xu Youzhi. He chuckles and, to her surprise, says with a pat on her shoulder: "My child, you are a dear. But the rhododendrons, in my view, is a symbol of love. Look at how independent it is, detached and aloof, growing and blooming where you least expect it to, where even pine trees cannot survive. Like the snow lotus, it is hardy at high altitudes and in extreme cold, but it is even more magnificent and devoted than the snow lotus..."

He breaks off suddenly. Now he is remembering when he carried Gu Long, who was injured in a fall, into the hut. The hut was now no longer the private world of just Meng Long and himself. So he walked out, never looking back. Gu Long, with his injured leg, called out from the hut: "Yun Long, come back!"

He heard it clearly but did not answer. Ahead of him the rhododendrons were ablaze with flowers, their fervor quickening his steps. Meng Long ran out to beg him to stay until Gu Long's injured leg healed. Then they could all go to Yan'an together. He refused, saying: "Give me up, Meng Long!"

The fact is he had given her up. He had

experienced that moment of ultimate glory, and that was enough for him, for it had given him enough strength to conquer a wider world. He no longer wished to go to Yan'an with her.

Little did he realize that what one gives up is often what becomes the most cherished. What he lost he would have to spend the rest of his life to find again. He feels he has stupidly spent so much money and enlisted the help of so many others to find out the whereabouts of his daughter. He could have come to the mainland himself to look. Maybe that's destiny. He walked away years ago when the rhododendrons were in full bloom; now he has come back amid blossoming rhododendrons. Forty years later, the mountains still stand and the flowers still bloom.

As his mind wanders he seems to see Gu Long waiting for him in the mud hut. His arms hugging his injured leg, he is saying: "Yun Long, so you are back?"

Leaving Rulan behind, he hurries into the empty hut, crying out in a hoarse voice: "Gu Long!"

There is no reply—although there is straw on the floor, yak horns on the wall, and signs of human habitation.

7

A glint of something blue and white in the dried straw catches Rulan's eye. When she takes a closer look she finds that it is her own hair clip. She probably dropped it last night in a careless moment. The instinct to pick it up is checked by the worry that with other people in the room, the risk of being caught in the act is great and she would have a hard time explaining herself. So she places her foot unobtrusively near the object and quietly flattens the straw over it, making sure the clip is buried out of sight.

The furtive maneuver flusters her and a slight flush rises in her face. But nobody is paying attention to her, not even Songlin. As she breathes with relief and the color fades from her face, she is suddenly overtaken by a sense of loss. She feels that by kicking the straw over the hair clip, she has buried everything that happened last night.

What is love? Such an elusive subject may not be worth the devotion of too much of one's time. She has been seriously looking for love for dozens of years and come up empty-handed. Until last night, when she took that important plunge. Was that love? She doesn't know; she is a little puzzled but at the same time she feels relief, relaxation and a happiness that soothes the heart. Maybe that's what love is all about. Mr. Xu speaks from experience when he says love stands off on its own; it can't be explained rationally.

How far her relationship with Chen Songlin will go in the future, she has no idea. They have not sworn themselves to eternal love. It's not a relationship sanctified by law. Maybe he loves her very much but maybe she is just one more conquest, a trophy that attests to his masculine prowess. Yet another possibility is that he had a fleeting illusion of loving her. Still she has no regret. The moment of mutual giving of affection, of each to the other, is, for her, everything.

But she can almost be sure of one thing: Chen Songlin cannot possibly love her forever. They are bound to part ways. And as a woman, no matter how unconventional she is, she is not immune to the desire for something she can always count on—support for all her life, an affection that has substance and that she can lay permanent claim to. She may break her heart over him but will not demand from him any type of firm commitment. The beauty of love lies in it incompleteness. For love is such a delicate, free spirit; anything absolute or definite will sap its exuberance and vitality.

If Semo's legendary magic mirror had not been shattered, there would not have been the unsurpassed beauty of Jiuzhaigou. Fragmentation has a beauty of its own, and life is often composed of broken fragments: broken love, broken family, broken prospects. It's a sad, tragic kind of beauty. Perhaps that's why people sometimes prefer a little ugliness to beauty.

As Rulan slowly walks out of the hut thinking these thoughts, she feels a sudden regret at having to leave. She'll probably never again come back to this little mud hut near the crest of the mountain. Flowers will bloom and flowers will wilt. She can only hope that these blooming rhododendrons will carry on her pursuit of a dream. She glances over her shoulder for one last look.

At this time Songlin also emerges from the hut, followed by Xing Xing, Sha Sha, and finally, Xu Youzhi.

8

At the door, Xu Youzhi does not look back but instead gazes up at the sky, as if listening for something, expecting something.

The sky is an azure blue, a blue peculiar to the highland, but it does not appear to be a great distance away. The clouds, too, appear very close, so close you think you can reach out and touch them with your hand. They are like a mass of rich, soft cotton wool, or a cluster of shapes and forms embodying human emotions.

He can't shake off the feeling that Gu Long is close by. Yes, when the clouds are so close, how can people be far away? He has traveled thousands of miles from across the Strait and now that he is so close to home, there is no reason he can't wait a little longer. He can't leave so soon. He must wait a while longer. He waits, expects and listens, hoping to hear once again that cry carried down from the far snow peaks: "Ah Long—"

But in place of the expected call there is only

silence. He sees a cloud of the highland; it silently alights on his face. His body, strong and solid like a mountain, sways—and collapses in another heart attack!

9

Xing Xing promptly opens the backpack. They lost the oxygen pouch when they were busy resuscitating him in Huanglong Ravine, but there is medicine in an inside pocket in the backpack. She unzips the pocket and sticks her hand in. She is a good organizer, so the small packets of heart medicine should be in there within easy reach.

But to her surprise the pocket is empty. Xing Xing feels her heart sink: did she leave the medicines on the desk in the hotel room?

No, not possible! He didn't take any medication while in the hotel, so the medicine never left the bag.

What happened? She rummages through the backpack and finally turns it upside down to empty the contents. Scattered on the floor are a tube of toothpaste, a toothbrush and a bottle of face cream but no medicine!

Chen Songlin says: "Don't panic! Try to remember if you put it somewhere else."

She turns out all her pockets and there's still no sign of it! Xing Xing suddenly remembers that before departure Xu Youzhi said she'd packed too many things. So without consulting her, he went ahead and removed bags of pork jerky, cookies and pistachios, and threw them in the waste basket of the hotel room, grumbling as he did so: "Were you planning to carry all this stuff home?" She winced as the stuff she so treasured went into the trash but dared not protest. He could very well have thrown away his own medicine with the rest.

There's nothing to do but instruct the driver to start the bus and take them downhill toward lower altitudes where more oxygen is available, and then, as soon as possible, to a hospital.

The driver does his best in negotiating the dangerous steep switchbacks as they come down the mountain highway, and it takes only an hour for them to arrive at the Fu Yuan Building in Huanglong Ravine, 1,000 meters lower in altitude. But Xu Youzhi remains unconscious. Feeling his pulse, Chen Songlin finds an angry, erratic drumbeat, now fast now slow. The people inside anxiously urge the driver to go faster but he slows down instead.

"What's the matter?" Chen Songlin sticks his head out of the window and sees, in the light of the setting sun, a few Tibetans slowly moving a herd of yaks along the road. The lead yak has a bronze bell around its neck; the bell makes a crisp, pleasant tinkle with each step the yak takes.

Xing Xing cries anxiously: "Someone go down and tell them to move the yaks to the side of the road."

Rulan springs to life, and before the car comes to a complete stop she is already at the door. "I'll get off and tell them!"

Songlin agitates his hand in warning, saying: "No, no! Once you stop, someone might ask for a ride. Then we'll never be able to get out of here."

True enough, as soon as the bus comes to a halt, the herders throng around the vehicle. One man, who wears his braided hair coiled around the top of his head, a robe bunched about his waist, and red tassels at his ears, is pounding on the door. There's nothing to do but open the door. This agile, muscular young fellow is carrying a gun, striking awe among the passengers even before he utters a word.

Rulan tries to explain that there is a very sick person on board, but he ignores her and self-importantly demands in Mandarin to see their identification. Xing Xing and Rulan quickly produce their respective ID cards, while Songlin retrieves from Xu Youzhi's pocket a travel document issued exclusively to visitors from Taiwan and hands it over. The man with the gun becomes very courteous now and gives back their papers after a cursory glance. He gets off the bus and waves them on after closing the door. He even goes to the front to move the yaks out of the way.

The bus now moves at full speed again as if in a race with the setting sun. As the altitude continues to fall, the passengers find breathing much easier and all symptoms of discomfort disappear. But Xu Youzhi does not show the least bit of improvement; on the contrary his face has turned paler. Even Sha Sha, normally a happy-go-lucky girl, is very worried and on the verge of tears. "It's all my fault. I shouldn't have gone looking for that Gu Long!"

"Don't say that," says Rulan, gently taking her hand. "We can only chalk it up to fate."

"Fate?" Sha Sha stares at her. "You believe in fate

too?"

After a slight pause, Rulan replies: "People...
Rather, I mean, women should believe in fate."

"Not me. I don't believe in fate!" Xing Xing
interjects vehemently and leans forward in a sudden
movement to rest her hands on the driver's seatback,
imploring: "Please drive faster, faster!"

The swift-flowing Fu River comes once again
into view.

South of the highway, the Fu River flows from
west to east, its water leaping and swirling downriver,
the constant rush throbbing with life.

Glancing at his watch, Chen Songlin estimates
their arrival time in the county town of Pingwu will
be at sunset, and the bus can go no faster. He cranks
the window half open, hoping the mountain wind
carrying refreshing oxygen across the river will help
invigorate the critically ill patient.

But Xu Youzhi's pulse is getting more erratic
and weaker. While Xing Xing keeps calling his name
softly, he shows no response. The vehicle comes to
another halt—it turns out they are back at the spot
where they were stopped earlier by the landslide. The
mud and rocks piled in the middle of the road once

again block their way.

"Let's take a detour over those shallows!" Songlin says after making a mental assessment of the situation. To the north of the Fu River and south of the road lies a length of dry riverbed strewn with large rounded boulders and covered with wet sand and mud. They crossed the river at this spot previously on their way up the mountain when they were cut off by the mudslide.

To their surprise, the shallows, which were quiet and deserted the last time they forded them, now teem with a motley crowd: men and women, old and young, people of various ethnicities in diverse garb. One wonders where they all came from. They seem to have fallen out of the sky to saturate this previously secluded open space.

They have no time to lose; no one cares about asking the people what they are doing. The bus turns off the road and lumbers down toward the shallows with its horn blasting. As they approach, they figure, those people will have to move aside to let the bus pass.

It turns out that despite the deafening honking of the horn the people do not even blink an eye but

keep on dredging the water and mud with their hands.
Only a few of the bare-bottomed kids cast a curious
glance at them but immediately go back to helping
the adults. No one is inclined to make way.

The bus is forced to stop and the young women
descend from the car to implore the crowd with
weepy voices: "I beg you! Please let us through—we
have a sick person inside. I beg you!"

But they are met with indifference; no one
deigns even to look at them. Xing Xing grabs the
arm of a stoutly built man, beseeching him to let the
car through, but is shoved aside and falls toward a
muddy puddle. Quickly the people working by the
water put protective arms around the utensils they've
been filling with mud and sand, afraid that she might
knock them over in her fall.

Chen Songlin helps Xing Xing up and points:
"See that boat?"

It is a small, crude steamboat, its drab hulk
lusterless even in the setting sun. Its only distinguishing
feature is a long steel arm that keeps lowering into the
water to dredge up mud and sand.

"Is it a dredger?" Xing Xing asks.

"No," Songlin shakes his head with a grave

expression, "it is a gold-digging boat—these people are gold-diggers."

"What can we do then?" Xing Xing is in despair.

"Let's move him out of the car," Rulan suggests. "We'll wave down a car on the highway once we cross to the other side."

That seems to be the only option left.

10

Lying in a jury-rigged stretcher hastily put together, Xu Youzhi thinks he's once again seeing a sun at the earliest stage of its rise. It is spat out by the line of snow peaks, like the yolk of a duck egg: fresh, round and mellow, its soft light an apricot pink, soothing and calming. But then he feels a sudden burning. The sun is now probably high in the sky, he thinks—the sun is at its gentlest only at sunrise and sunset. When it hangs high in the sky, it is incandescent and strong and forbidden to naked human eyes.

As these thoughts parade through his mind, the sun disappears. Suddenly he sees a rock face of a bright red color standing tall in the dim light of the dusk. Fixing his gaze on the rock face, he seems to see mountains, rivers and people. Bands of people are embroiled in mortal combat, kicking up a storm that causes the rock to sway—there's no clear winner in the fight.

It is bitterly cold and he appears to be on his feet, looking out from a sheer cliff on a snow peak. He is eager to leave because his legs are frozen stiff, but his interest has been whetted and he decides to stay despite the bitter cold. Then the revelation comes to him: in these struggles it is always the old guard that is defeated by the newcomers, who in turn are defeated by newer comers, who are then defeated by the newest comers, and so the cycle goes on.

As he rejoices at this discovery, he feels a sudden pat on the shoulder. "Brother, so you are here too?"

He winces and looks up. The man's face looks very familiar but he can't at the moment put a name to it. The man talks to him like an old acquaintance, and he is embarrassed to ask for his name, so he just chuckles: "Heh heh, I was just watching..."

"Did you see yourself in it?" the man asks casually.

"Me?" He is astonished. "You mean I am in that

picture?"

"Of course," the man says with absolute certainty. "It is a history, with all of us in it." As if to prove his point, he points, saying: "Look! That's me there."

Following the direction of his hand, Xu Youzhi sees a large band of armed people giving chase to a silhouette. Then it dawns on him. "Gu Long! My brother Gu Long! I've looked long and hard for you! Now tell me where our Meng Long is."

"Meng Long?" The man points in the general direction of the rock face: "There, over there!"

"But where?" Rubbing his eyes repeatedly, Xu Youzhi sees only a blur of milling silhouettes. "Which one is Meng Long? Why can't I make her out?"

"Oh, my brother, why are you taking it so seriously?" the man asks disapprovingly. "The history of a country, a nation, is but a wisp of smoke that blows away in the blink of an eye. Human lives are so insignificant. Nobody can claim to see things in absolute clarity. Most see only a hazy outline."

"Is that so?" Xu Youzhi nods with slow understanding but he is unprepared to let go just yet. "What about my daughter? Where is she? Don't tell me she is also a hazy outline."

With a laugh, the man stabs a finger at Xu Youzhi's chest. "She's your daughter. She has your blood and carries your genes. Why are you asking anyone else but yourself?"

Xu Youzhi winces and then painfully clutches at his own chest. "You mean I abandoned my own daughter? And I have done her wrong? Yes, it's true, I did abandon her and wrong her. But I...I have not forgotten her. I love her and not a moment passes without my thinking of her. It's true, I miss her all the time, wanting to hug her, kiss her and buy dolls for her. I want her to support me when I am too old to walk by myself and to push me in a wheelchair when I am no longer mobile. I think...I even think that if she had been with me all this time I would not love her and miss her as much as I do. My...my daughter, where are you? Where are you?"

"She is right in there!" The man stabs an emphatic finger at his heart.

His body feels as if it had been split open by a sharp sword, with his heart broken in halves. The rock face disappears. Gu Long has vanished, having been dragged by someone into a dark abyss. He clings tightly to a shrub on the vertical face of the cliff, struggling desperately. "No, no, I want to see my daughter, my daughter!"

Suddenly there is a flash of white light before his eyes. It is at first very weak, like the pale morning light of early dawn, then it expands and grows. He finds himself catapulted out of the abyss and walking among mountains capped by pure white snow.

Above the snow peaks is an azure sky, so close to the mountains that he could ascend into the blue sky simply by walking along the line of peaks. He walks toward the sky, feeling that all pain has left his body, which is almost weightless now. Then he sees his late mother, who beckons from the heavens, wearing a traditional dress, with a slant front opening, made of homespun cloth dyed in blue with a pattern of white flowers.

He calls out to her, remembering that he wasn't able to come to her funeral and wasn't able to even send a letter or remit money. All he could do from across the Strait was sing over and over, as the tears poured: "We'll meet again, meet again, let's meet again in heaven…"

"Mama!" he cries again with sorrow. "I have not been a dutiful son!"

But his mother looks at him and smiles. She glitters with a fantastic brilliance and she smiles her tender maternal smile. "My child! Come with me! Listen! We'll meet again, meet again, let's meet again in heaven..."

It's as if the sun, the moon and the stars were singing in chorus, with every ray of light in the vast, boundless firmament carrying the melody of the tune.

His heart is filled with a sweet serenity. He feels he has been fused with the blue rays of the universe, fused with the melody. He is the universe, he is the song, his daughter must be with him.

When the last rays of sunset are buried in the roaring, frothing Fu River, the teeming gold-digging crowds are still working feverishly. Meanwhile, on the stretcher Xu Youzhi is failing, his two hands clawing at the air. Suddenly he grasps Rulan.

The grasp is so tight that Rulan's delicate hand can barely move in his big, fleshy palm. She no longer tries to free her hand but leaves it in his grip. With her free hand she wipes off the saliva from the corners of his mouth. She doesn't know why she is doing this. In the eyes of the others, the scene strongly suggests that of a mother wiping off her baby's mouth. No one can guess that deep in her heart, she fervently wishes he could open his eyes and, one more time, call her: "My child!"

But he never again opens his eyes or utters a word. The hand that grasps hers becomes progressively colder and stiffer, but also tighter, so tight that it seems to want to break through her skin and tap into her veins.

Withstanding the pain, she looks at him, thinking to herself: "What kind of thing is fate?" This rich executive from Taiwan has a wife and family, a thriving business, and so much money he would never be able to spend it all in one lifetime. But in his last moments he has clutched at her hand—the hand of a woman from mainland China whom he recently met for the first time. And she herself, what will she be able to hold onto in the last moments of her life?

As she thinks those thoughts, two transparent tears roll out of her eyes.

Stories by Contemporary Writers from Shanghai

The Little Restaurant
Wang Anyi

A Pair of Jade Frogs
Ye Xin

Forty Roses
Sun Yong

Goodby, Xu Hu!
Zhao Changtian

Vicissitudes of Life
Wang Xiaoying

The Elephant
Chen Cun

Folk Song
Li Xiao

The Messenger's Letter
Sun Ganlu

Ah, Blue Bird
Lu Xing'er

His One and Only
Wang Xiaoyu

When a Baby Is Born
Cheng Naishan

Dissipation
Tang Ying

Paradise on Earth
Zhu Lin

The Most Beautiful Face in the World
Xue Shu

Beautiful Days
Teng Xiaolan